S0-AFD-526

She closed her eyes and waited... waited....

"Am I supposed to kiss you now, Anne-Marie?" he said raggedly.

She'd have been humiliated beyond endurance if she hadn't detected the torment behind his remark. "How about a little truth for a change, Ethan? How about 'I want to kiss you, Anne-Marie'?" she said.

"No," he muttered. But his hands betrayed him and slid through her hair. "No," he said again, almost savagely. "It'll never happen."

"Why not?"

"Because it would be a mistake."

But either he didn't really believe what he was saying or he, too, was at the mercy of impulses beyond his control, because his head dipped lower and his lips searched out hers. Their imprint scorched her and left her melting against him. At length he broke all contact and stepped back. "I was right," he said hoarsely. "That was a big mistake."

"Sometimes people can learn a great deal from their mistakes," she said.

*Passion*™

in

Harlequin Presents®

Looking for sophisticated stories that **sizzle**?
Wanting a read that has a little extra **spice**?

Sinful Truths
by
Anne Mather

On sale in September, #2344

Pick up a Presents *Passion*™ novel—
where **seduction** is *guaranteed!*

Available only from Harlequin Presents®

Catherine Spencer

IN THE BEST MAN'S BED

Passion™

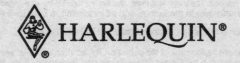

TORONTO • NEW YORK • LONDON
AMSTERDAM • PARIS • SYDNEY • HAMBURG
STOCKHOLM • ATHENS • TOKYO • MILAN • MADRID
PRAGUE • WARSAW • BUDAPEST • AUCKLAND

If you purchased this book without a cover you should be aware
that this book is stolen property. It was reported as "unsold and
destroyed" to the publisher, and neither the author nor the
publisher has received any payment for this "stripped book."

ISBN 0-373-12341-8

IN THE BEST MAN'S BED

First North American Publication 2003.

Copyright © 2003 by Kathy Garner.

All rights reserved. Except for use in any review, the reproduction or
utilization of this work in whole or in part in any form by any electronic,
mechanical or other means, now known or hereafter invented, including
xerography, photocopying and recording, or in any information storage
or retrieval system, is forbidden without the written permission of the
publisher, Harlequin Enterprises Limited, 225 Duncan Mill Road,
Don Mills, Ontario, Canada M3B 3K9.

All characters in this book have no existence outside the imagination of
the author and have no relation whatsoever to anyone bearing the same
name or names. They are not even distantly inspired by any individual
known or unknown to the author, and all incidents are pure invention.

This edition published by arrangement with Harlequin Books S.A.

® and TM are trademarks of the publisher. Trademarks indicated with
® are registered in the United States Patent and Trademark Office, the
Canadian Trade Marks Office and in other countries.

Visit us at www.eHarlequin.com

Printed in U.S.A.

CHAPTER ONE

ETHAN BEAUMONT...Ethan Andrew Beaumont...Monsieur Beaumont. Ever since the wedding date had been set, his was the name on everyone's lips; his was the name uttered with the kind of reverence normally accorded only to royalty, popes or dictators.

So given that it's Philippe Beaumont who's marrying my best friend, what's wrong with this picture? Anne-Marie Barclay wondered, sipping thoughtfully at her champagne. *Why is it that, where other people's weddings are concerned, the bride and groom take center stage, but in this instance, it's all about Ethan Beaumont? And why is Solange allowing it?*

"If you look just beyond the tip of the starboard wing, *Mademoiselle,* you'll catch your first glimpse of Bellefleur." Moving with surprising stealth and grace for such a big man, the flight attendant materialized from the galley at the rear of the private jet, and pointed over Anne-Marie's shoulder. "It's the island shaped like a crescent moon."

She craned her neck and scanned the specks of land floating like emerald gems on the sapphire-blue water, thousands of feet below. "Yes, I see it," she said, and wondered why the sight of the island, tranquil and beautiful even from this distance, should fill her with such odd apprehension. "How long before we land?"

"We'll begin our descent shortly. Please remain seated and keep your seat belt fastened." His smile flashed brilliant white in his ebony face. "Not that you need to be

5

reminded. You haven't moved since we left the mainland. Are you by chance a nervous flyer, *Mademoiselle?*"

"Not as a rule." She glanced again out of the window and found nothing but blue sky beyond, as the jet banked in a steep turn. "But nor do I usually travel in so small an aircraft." *Especially not over miles of open water.*

He smiled again, kindly. "You're in excellent hands. Captain Morgan is a most capable pilot. *Monsieur* Beaumont hires only the best."

There it was again, the Beaumont name rolling off the steward's tongue with lilting Caribbean reverence, as if her host ranked head and shoulders above other mortals. And again Anne-Marie felt that disturbing little surge of misgiving. She was not looking forward to meeting the almighty *Monsieur* Beaumont.

"He's nothing like Philippe, although there's quite a strong family resemblance, even though they're only half brothers," Solange had told her, when she phoned with news of the forthcoming wedding. "He's larger in every respect. Larger than life, almost, and certainly lord of all he surveys. They practically curtsy to him when he passes through the town. I can see why Philippe was a little anxious about breaking news of our engagement to him. Ethan can be…how shall I put it? *Un peu formidable.*"

"In other words, he's a tyrant." Anne-Marie had rolled her eyes in disbelief. "Imagine a grown man being afraid to tell his family that he's getting married. It's positively medieval! If you ask me, all that wealth and power has gone to the formidable Ethan Beaumont's head."

A thoughtful pause followed before Solange replied, "*Oui,* he is powerful, but underneath it all, he's a very good man. Not cuddly like *mon cher* teddy bear, of course—he's much too distant for that. I can't imagine him ever allowing grand passion to rule the day."

"He did, at least once," Anne-Marie pointed out. "He's got a son to prove it."

"But alas, no wife. Maybe he inherited too much English reserve from his mother, and that's why his marriage lasted so short a time." Solange sighed, and Anne-Marie had imagined her shrugging in that uniquely French way of hers. "Such a pity! Such a waste!"

"Such a blessing, you mean! No woman needs the kind of man in her life who'd deprive her of her child. I feel sorry for the little boy, being at the mercy of such a father."

"But that was not Ethan's fault, Anne-Marie! The mother chose to leave both her husband and her son."

"Which just goes to show how bad things must have been for her, that she'd give up her baby rather than put up with the husband!"

Solange's initial burst of laughter, rippling over the phone like music, had dwindled into hushed alarm, as if she were afraid she'd be sent to her room without dinner for disturbing the peace. "It's all right to say such audacious things to me in private, but you must take care not to speak so in front of other people when you join me on Bellefleur. They would not take kindly to a stranger criticizing their *Seigneur*."

Seigneur, indeed! Anne-Marie leaned back in her seat and closed her eyes as the blue Caribbean Sea rushed up to meet the jet on its final approach to the island. How feudal—and how utterly absurd!

Feudal, perhaps, but her notions of absurdity wavered alarmingly during the journey from the airport to the Beaumont estate. Seated in solitary splendor in the back of a black Mercedes limousine, she experienced instead the unsettling sense that *she* was the only anomaly on Bellefleur.

As the chauffeur-driven car rolled sedately through the winding streets of the small town, residents stopped to acknowledge its passing with a respectful nod which came close to a bow. Dark-eyed children waved chubby hands.

Should she wave back? she wondered, hating the sudden uncertainty usurping her normal self-confidence, *or wouldn't the Seigneur approve?*

Probably not!

"He'll be very charming, very attentive to your comfort and needs, but don't expect him to treat you the way a North American host would," Solange had warned. "He's much too reserved for that. He'll probably call you *Mademoiselle* Barclay, the entire time you're here. It took him ages to unbend enough to call me by my first name."

When she'd descended the steps from the jet and set foot on the tarmac, the sun's shimmering heat had hit Anne-Marie like a wall, and she'd been glad to take refuge in the dim, air-conditioned comfort of the Mercedes. But as the vehicle left the town behind and climbed the hill leading to the Beaumont estate, her friend's warning settled unpleasantly in the pit of her stomach like a too-large meal of badly prepared food.

More than a month of having to bow and scrape to some domineering individual given to feudal delusions of grandeur was enough to kill anyone's appetite! Worse, it promised to leach all the pleasure out of her coming to Bellefleur to be her best friend's maid of honor, and instead threatened to turn the visit into a penance for sins not yet committed.

That an autocratic stranger should wield such power that he cast a pall over Solange's wedding was indefensible. But more troubling by far, in Anne-Marie's opinion, was the fear that his domination would spill over and influence the marriage, as well.

She had met Philippe Beaumont, and liked him. He and Solange were well-matched. But he'd never struck Anne-Marie as a particularly strong or forceful man. Given a choice, he'd choose the easy route over the difficult, and whether he'd be any match for his assertive half brother seemed questionable, given what she knew about the latter.

Her concerns intensified as the Mercedes swept through the gates guarding the entrance to the family estate and, a short time later, drew up in the forecourt of the main house.

She was no stranger to luxury. She'd attended the best schools, seen something of the world, never known what it was to lack money or material comforts. Yet, quite apart from its architectural beauty, the sheer size and opulence of the Beaumont mansion overwhelmed her.

She'd heard that royalty had slept under its roofs and she could well believe it. This was no mere villa, no rich man's private island hideaway. This was a palace which, surrounded though it might be with smothering tropical heat, nevertheless exuded an intimidating aura of cool, dignified formality. If it was representational of its owner, then small wonder Solange held him in such awe.

"Mademoiselle?"

With a start, Anne-Marie realized the passenger door stood open, and a manservant, immaculate in starched white Bermuda shorts and tailored, short-sleeved white shirt, waited to hand her out of the car. Bracing herself to cope with whatever situation might await her, she slid across the leather seat and stepped into the courtyard.

Somehow, that made all the difference to her perceptions. Everywhere she looked, she saw flowers. But rather than viewing them from behind the tinted windows of the

Mercedes, her eyes were assaulted by the splendor of color spilling over cream stucco walls, and tumbling from huge stone jardinieres in a riot of purple and scarlet and bright orange.

She became instantly aware of the cooling splash of fountains, and the raucous shriek of brilliantly feathered birds; of the exotic scent of gardenias; of ginger blossom and plumeria.

Shading her from the sun with an exquisitely painted parasol, the manservant escorted her up a shallow flight of steps and into the building—not by way of a front door because, for all its luxury, the villa didn't appear to possess one. Instead, a pair of curved iron gates, so delicately wrought that they resembled black lace, led directly to a covered inner courtyard, circular in shape and large enough to serve as a ballroom.

Solange waited there, her dark eyes liquid with emotion, her smile tremulous. "Oh, how I've missed you!" she exclaimed softly, gliding forward over the marble-tiled floor, and kissing Anne-Marie on both cheeks. "Welcome to Bellefleur, *ma chère, chère amie!* I'm so glad to have you here at last!"

"Glad?" A little teary-eyed herself, Anne-Marie held her friend at arm's length and inspected her searchingly. "If you're so glad, why are you crying?"

"Because I'm happy."

"You don't look happy, Solange."

Solange gave her little Gallic shrug, cast a furtive glance over her shoulder, and said, "Come, let me show you where you'll be sleeping. We can talk more freely there. Ethan instructed the staff to put you in the guest pavilion next to mine."

"You mean to say you're not staying here in the house?"

"Not until I'm a married woman. Ethan wouldn't approve. Philippe might be tempted to sneak into my bed at night."

"The way he did when you were still living in Paris, you mean?"

"Hush!" Solange pressed a nervous finger to her lips. "No one must know that, Anne-Marie. Standards are different here."

"So I gathered," she muttered, following Solange through another curved gateway on the opposite side of the foyer, to a paved terrace overlooking an enormous, infinity-edged pool. The view beyond was breathtaking; a sweeping panorama of sky and sea framed with swaying coconut palms and poinciana trees. "Tell me, do the guest pavilions have doors and windows, or must we whisper all the time we're there, as well, in case anyone overhears?"

"We'll be quite private, except for when our maids are present. Then we must be discreet." She led the way down a shady path which wound among a series of ponds connected to each other by miniature waterfalls and pebbled, man-made streams. "We're a good distance from the main house, as you'll see, but the suites are very luxurious and spacious."

"That's good. I'll need plenty of room to finish working on the dresses."

Solange flung a glance over her shoulder and, just for a moment, her usual vivacity showed in her face. "I can hardly wait to see mine. The drawings you sent were gorgeous."

"We can have a fitting later on, if you like, to give you an idea of how you're going to look in the finished product."

"It'll have to wait until tomorrow. Because you've been

traveling all day, we're having an early dinner, and I expect you'll want to shower and change first.''

"Presumably, I'll be meeting the formidable Ethan Beaumont.'' Anne-Marie grimaced. "I've got indigestion already!''

"Not tonight, you won't,'' Solange said with a laugh. "I ordered a private meal to be delivered to my suite. Ethan's aunt and uncle are visiting friends until tomorrow afternoon, and he's away on business.''

"I understood running this island and the lives of everyone on it was his business.''

"*Mon Dieu, non!* He has investment and real estate portfolios all over the world, though he's recently begun delegating Philippe to take charge of them, and concentrating all his energy on his oil interests. That's what's taken him away this time.''

"To the Middle East? Good! The farther away he is, the better! I already dislike the man and I'm in no hurry to meet him.''

"Oh, he's much closer than the Middle East, I'm afraid. Just off the coast of Venezuela, in fact, which is no great distance from here at all. He'll be back in a few days, I'm sure, but until then you'll have to make do with his aunt and uncle, who also live on the estate, and with Adrian.''

"Who's Adrian?''

"Ethan's son.'' Her voice softened. "He's an adorable little boy. I don't think you'll find being around him a very great hardship, regardless of how you feel about his father.''

The path opened onto a wide expanse of lawn just then, and she stopped to point out a pair of villas perched high above the sea. "Well, here we are, *chérie*. This where we'll be living for the next little while.''

Given her first impressions of the Beaumont estate,

Anne-Marie ought not to have been surprised by the sight confronting her now. Surrounded by showy flower beds, and separated from each other by a covered walkway, the villas were miniature replicas of the main house, with the same deep verandahs, lacy iron French doors, and a smaller version of the infinity-edged swimming pool.

"I have to say that, whatever else his shortcomings, your future brother-in-law knows how to treat guests," she exclaimed, captivated by the serene elegance of the setting. "This is paradise, Solange. Perfection! We're going to have a lot of fun here over the next few weeks."

Solange smiled wistfully. "I hope you're right."

"There shouldn't be any question but that I am! The days leading up to the wedding are supposed to be a happy time for the bride, and I don't understand why you're not glowing with your usual radiance. What is it, Solange? Are you having doubts about marrying Philippe? Because if you are, it's not too late to call the whole thing off."

"Oh, it's not Philippe! I adore him, more than ever, and I'm always happy when he's with me. But the rest of the time…" Her mouth drooped sadly. "…it seems so foreign here."

"How can it be foreign? It might be a long way from Paris, but it's still French. Imagine how much worse it would be if everyone spoke Spanish or Portuguese, and you couldn't understand a word they were saying."

"Perhaps what I should have said is that, even though the language is familiar, I feel like a foreigner." She gestured at the lush spread of land stretching to either side, and the jungle-clad hill rising behind the estate. "There are two kinds of people on this island, Anne-Marie: those who belong because they were born here, and the rest of us, who weren't."

"If that's true, how are you going to cope with living here?"

"Philippe tells me that once we're married and start a family, I'll feel differently. I'll be accepted. Maybe he's right. Maybe it's just that I've been alone too much lately."

"Why hasn't Philippe been with you?"

"He's been taking care of business in Europe, and Asia. Right now, he's in Vienna and has been for the last week. Ethan says that since he'll soon be a married man, he has to take a more active role in the family business."

Ethan says, Ethan thinks, Ethan decrees...!

"Tell me Solange, has anyone ever dared to say, to hell with what Ethan wants?"

Solange rolled her eyes like a frightened foal caught in quicksand. "*Mon Dieu,* don't ever say something like that in front of anyone else! It would be considered...." She fluttered her hands, groping for the right word.

"Treason?" Anne-Marie supplied witheringly. "Good grief, girlfriend, who is this browbeaten little creature reciting the party line with every breath? What's happened to the woman I used to know?"

"I'm still the same inside." Solange squared her shoulders and made a determined effort to look more cheerful. "I've just had a little difficulty adjusting to my new situation. But now that you're here, I'll soon be my old self again."

They'd reached the guest houses by then, and looking through the open entrance to the one she'd been assigned to, Anne-Marie saw that her luggage had been delivered and that a maid was busily unpacking her suitcases.

"I don't want her messing around with the wedding outfits, so I'd better get in there and take charge before the hired help starts on the travel trunk," she said. "But this conversation is far from over, Solange. You might fool everyone else with your polite, subdued little smile, and your docile acceptance of the all-important *rules,* but you aren't fooling me. Something's not quite right in paradise, and I intend to find out what it is.''

"It's nothing—just pre-wedding nerves and difficulty settling into a new situation," Solange insisted, edging nervously toward her own suite. "I've always been shy, you know that, and it's all taking a bit of getting used to, especially with Philippe away so much. I suppose, if truth be told, I'm just plain lonely."

Small wonder! Anne-Marie thought. *And that's something else we can thank the almighty Ethan Andrew Beaumont Lewis for!*

She thought she'd sleep late the next morning, but even though she'd fallen into bed exhausted the night before, Anne-Marie awoke at sunrise. It would be hours before breakfast was served, but after last night's dinner, she needed exercise more than food, especially if she wanted to fit into the dress she'd be wearing at the wedding.

"Always assuming," she murmured, slipping between the folds of filmy mosquito netting draped around the bed, and hunting through the dresser drawers for a bikini, "that the wedding takes place which, from everything I've surmised, might not happen if the lord and master has his way."

The pool glimmered invitingly when she looked outside, but there was no sign of life from Solange's villa, which was probably a good thing. She'd looked very pale and hollow-eyed by the time dinner was over, as if she hadn't been getting enough sleep, and could probably use a few more hours of rest.

Better not to disturb her, Anne-Marie decided, pulling a

cover-up over her bikini and slinging her camera around her neck. Hiking down the hill to wade in the milk-warm Caribbean would serve just as well as a dip in the pool.

Finding a way down to the beach turned out to be a more frustrating experience than she'd expected, though. Even in the bright light of midday, many of the paths winding through the estate gardens lay in the protective shade of trees. At that hour of the morning, with the sun still not high enough to penetrate the dense green canopy overhead, she found it almost impossible to keep track of the direction she took.

Twice, she ended up back where she'd begun. Another time, she found herself on the edge of the cliff, with a sheer drop down to the shore. Finally, when she was so confused that she wasn't certain she'd even find her way back to her villa, she came across a man tending one of the ponds.

He knelt with his back to her, and her first thought was that he must have spent most of his life toiling in the hot sun for Ethan Beaumont. How else would he have developed such a physique, or his skin acquired such a deep and glowing tan? And who else but a manual laborer would be allowed to wander about the estate wearing nothing but faded denim cutoffs?

"Bonjour," she began, unsure of the protocol involved in approaching a gardener—because whatever else she might have missed at dinner the previous evening, she'd quickly learned that, with regard to the house staff, protocol was paramount. The wine steward did not refill the water goblets; the butler who served the food did not remove the empty plates.

That being the case, it was entirely possible that this lowly employee with his face practically submersed in the pond, might not be allowed to speak to guests. Certainly, the way he ignored her greeting suggested as much—unless he was deaf or didn't understand her French.

"Excusez moi," she said, stepping closer and speaking a little louder. *"S'il vous plait, monsieur—"*

Irritably, he flapped his hand at her and, in case she hadn't understood the message *that* was supposed to convey, said curtly, "Lower your voice. I heard you the first time."

His English might be flawless, albeit slightly accented, but his manner left a great deal to be desired. Offended, she snapped, "Really? And how do you suppose your employer would react, if he knew how rude you were to one of his guests?"

"Disturbed," he replied, still bent double over the pond. "But not nearly as disturbed as he'd be with the guest for interfering with the delicate business of keeping his prize koi alive and well."

"You're the fish man?"

The way his broad shoulders sort of rippled and shook at the question made her wonder if he was having some sort of fit. "You could call me that, I suppose."

"What does your employer call you?"

"Nothing," he said carelessly. "He's never conferred a title on me. In his eyes, I'm not important enough to warrant one."

"Yet you continue to work here. You must love what you do, to put up with that sort of abuse."

"Oh yes, lady," he replied, his deep baritone suddenly adopting a musical Caribbean lilt. "Master lets me feed and tend his fish. Gives me hut to live in, and rum to drink. Fish man very lucky guy."

"There's no need to be so offensive. It's not my fault if the work you do isn't properly appreciated." She tipped her head to one side, intrigued by his preoccupation with the task at hand. "Exactly what *is* it that you're doing?"

"An egret's had a go at the koi. I'm repairing the damage."

"I didn't know that was possible. How do you do it?"

"I get the fish to come to the surface so that I can treat their injuries."

"Of course you do," she said mockingly. "And because they're obedience trained, they stay put while you bandage them."

"Not quite. But they stick around long enough for me to disinfect the puncture wounds inflicted by the bird."

She stepped closer and saw that he wasn't exaggerating. One fish, over a foot long, was happily nibbling food pellets from one of his hands and, with the other, allowing him to dab some substance on the nasty-looking hole piercing its back.

"You really care about them, don't you?" she said, impressed despite herself.

"I respect them," he said. "Some are over fifty years old. They deserve to be well cared for. Is there a reason you're wandering around the gardens at this hour?"

"I'm looking for a way to get down to the beach. I'd like to go for a swim."

"What's wrong with the guest pool?"

"My friend's still sleeping and I don't want to disturb her. She hasn't had a very easy time of things lately."

"How so? Isn't she about to marry the man of her dreams?"

"It's the other man that's part of the package who's causing her grief."

He ran a caressing finger over the back of the fish he'd been tending. "There's another man in the picture? That hardly bodes well for the marriage."

"Not *that* kind of other man. But never mind. I shouldn't even be discussing the matter with you. *Monsieur* Beaumont wouldn't approve."

"No, *Monsieur* Beaumont certainly wouldn't," he said. "There isn't a path to the beach on this side of the property. If you want an early swim, I suggest you go up to the main house and use the pool there."

"Oh, I don't think so. It's probably against the rules for a guest to dip her toe in the family pool without invitation."

"You don't seem fond of the Beaumonts. Do you know them well?"

"Except for the bridegroom, hardly at all. I haven't even met the big cheese yet, but what I've heard hasn't exactly swept me off my feet."

He wiped his hands on the seat of his cutoffs, and jumped lithely to his feet. He was very tall. Very. "The big cheese will be crushed to hear that."

"Who's going to tell him—you?"

He laughed, and turned toward her just as the sun lifted over the side of the hill and afforded her first good look at him, and she almost cringed.

This was no common laborer! He had the face of an aristocrat, with high, elegantly carved cheekbones, and a mouth set in the lines of one unaccustomed to suffering fools gladly. His jaw, faintly shadowed, was lean, and his eyes, vivid beneath dark sweeping brows, the bluest she'd ever seen. And she didn't need an introduction to know his name.

"You don't work here!" she said, weakly.

"Certainly I do. Very hard, in fact."

"No, you don't, and you're not the fish man. You're Ethan Beaumont!"

He inclined his head. "And where is it written that I can't be both?"

Oh, rats! Talk about putting her foot in it! "Why didn't you say something sooner?"

"Because it was more informative listening to you running off at the mouth. Is there anything else you'd like to tell me about myself?"

"No," she mumbled, so embarrassed she wanted to die. "I don't have anything else to say right now."

"In that case, allow me to escort you up to the house where, at my invitation, you may swim in the pool to your heart's content."

"I don't think I feel like swimming anymore. I think I'll just go back to the guest house."

"And disturb the delicate bride-to-be? I won't hear of it." He towered over her and took her elbow in a not-to-be-thwarted grip. "Come along, *Mademoiselle.* Let's not waste any more time debating the issue. It's already been settled. By the big cheese."

CHAPTER TWO

"YOU'RE supposed to be digging for oil in Venezuela," she panted, struggling to keep up with his long-legged stride.

"We don't dig, we drill."

"You know what I mean!"

"Oh yes," he assured her, the seductive baritone of his voice laced with irony. "You have a way with words which leaves a man in little doubt about their meaning."

Although she'd sooner have poked hot needles in her eyes than offer an apology, she knew one was called for. "I'm afraid I was out of line, talking to you the way I did when I first saw you, and I'm sorry."

"You should be. Is it customary in your part of the world to criticize one's host to his employees?"

The distaste with which he said "your part of the world" made it sound as if she'd emerged from under a very unsavory rock. "No," she said. "But where I come from, hosts aren't usually so inhospitable. Nor do they go around impersonating other people."

"Inhospitable?" His sleekly elegant brows rose in mock surprise. "Your accommodation falls short of your expectations? The food is not to your liking? My staff have treated you discourteously?"

"Dinner was exquisite, your staff couldn't be kinder or more helpful, and my accommodation," she replied, thinking of the delicately fashioned iron four-poster bed with its Sea Island cotton sheets, and elegant draperies which more closely resembled silk wedding-veil tulle than mosquito netting, "is everything I could wish for. It's the atmosphere around here that leaves something to be desired."

"A sentiment which my future sister-in-law appears to share. Dare I ask why?"

"Let's just say she's hardly the poster child for bridal bliss, and leave it at that."

He held back the fronds of a giant fern and waited for her to pass by. Just there, the path was narrow, an iridescent green lane awash with the scent of the jungle, a thousand hidden flowers—and him.

He smelled of morning and cool water faintly kissed by the tropics. He oozed raw strength, the kind which defied the elements. He would neither wilt under the sun's heat, nor bend before the storms which swept over the island during hurricane season, and as long as she didn't look at him, she could prolong the illusion that he was exactly what she'd first assumed him to be: a subordinate born to the grinding, endless toil of working the cotton plantation or tending the gardens.

But one glance at the elegant conformation of bone and muscle underlying the gleaming skin, at the well-shaped hands, the patrician features, and most of all, at the intelligence in those cool, spectacular eyes, and she felt herself dwindle into insignificance. This was a giant of a man, not so much because of his size and physical beauty, which were considerable, but because of the innate bearing in his manner. The mantle of authority, of culture and refinement, sat easily on his shoulders.

"Please proceed," he said, waving her ahead with an imperious gesture. "And explain your last remark."

She scuttled past and muttered, "I've forgotten what it was."

"Then allow me to refresh your memory. You said you don't find Solange the picture of bridal bliss."

"Well, do *you?*"

"I hardly know her well enough to say."

"Oh, please! Even a complete stranger, if he bothered to take a good look at her, would see at once that she's anything but brimming over with happiness."

"She *has* struck me as moody and difficult to please." He gave a careless shrug. "Unfortunate traits in a woman about to become a wife, wouldn't you say?"

Irked by the casual way he'd pigeon-holed Solange without bothering to learn what was really causing her so much distress, Anne-Marie said tartly, "Almost as unfortunate as finding yourself related by marriage to a man so ready to assume the worst of you!"

"If I've misjudged her—"

"There's no 'if' about it! I've known Solange for over ten years and I can assure you she's normally the most equable woman in the world. But finding herself sequestered as far away from the main house as possible, as if she's carrying some horrible, contagious disease, doesn't do a whole lot for her self-esteem."

"I'm preserving her good reputation."

"You're isolating her and making her feel unwanted!"

"That's ridiculous," he said bluntly. "During the day, she's welcome to spend as much time as she likes with the rest of the family."

They'd reached the upper terrace by then. "She's too intimidated," Anne-Marie said, stopping to admire a bed of tall pink lilies with burgundy leaves. "She'd feel she was imposing, especially on those days when Philippe isn't there to run interference for her."

"If she thinks he'll constantly be at her side once they're married, she's in for a rude awakening. By his own choosing, Philippe has led a very carefree bachelor life up until now, and is no more equipped to be a husband than I am to tame a tiger. In order to fulfill his marital obligations, he'll be kept very busy learning to pull his own weight in the family business. And that, I'm afraid, will involve his spending a certain amount of time off the island.''

''Will it?'' she said heatedly. ''Or is this simply your way of sabotaging a marriage you don't approve of?''

His mouth curved in displeasure. ''I've never found it necessary to stoop to such underhand measures. If I don't like something, I make no secret of my intent to change it.''

Who did he think he was—God? ''And what if you can't?''

''There's always a way,'' he said impassively. ''It's simply a matter of finding it. But you may rest easy on one score at least. I take no pleasure in reducing innocent women to tears or despair. Whatever else might be upsetting Solange, she has nothing to fear from me. I have only her best interests at heart.''

''I'd like to believe that's the case.''

''I'm not in the habit of lying, *Mademoiselle*.''

He uttered the words with such a wealth of dignity that she was ashamed. No, he would not stoop to lying. Whatever his faults, he would never compromise his integrity.

He indicated the pool, stretching before them like an eighty-foot length of satin undulating in a whisper of breeze. ''Enjoy your swim. You look as if you need it. You're more than a little flushed.''

Hidden by the shadowed fretwork of the door opening onto his bedroom verandah, he watched her approach the shallow end of the pool, and cautiously lower herself over the side. In every other respect, she appeared to be exactly as he'd anticipated: brash, abrasive, and disagreeably self-confident, like most North American women.

It surprised him that she was so tentative in the water, and it annoyed him, too. He didn't want to be made aware of any vulnerability she might possess. Dealing with Solange's fragility was more than enough.

"Papa!" The door burst open and Adrian catapulted into the room. "When did you come home?"

"Last night," he said, scooping his son into his arms.

"You didn't kiss me good night!"

"Of course I did. But you were sleeping so soundly, you didn't know."

"I'm scared when you go away, Papa." The sweetly-rounded arms crept around his neck and held on tight. "What if you forgot to come home again?"

"Don't be scared, *mon petit*," he said. "Parents never forget to come back to their children."

"They do, sometimes. I heard *Tante* Josephine say that's why I don't have a mama."

Damn you, Lisa! Inwardly cursing his ex-wife, he said, "You'll always have me, son," and made a mental note to remind his aunt to watch her words around the boy.

Adrian wriggled to the floor and tugged at his hand. "Teach me to swim some more, Papa."

His glance slewed back to the pool. She'd ventured in a little farther and was floating on her back, with her hair fanned out around her head like the tentacles of a pale sea anemone. Just as well she wasn't expending much energy. Any sudden movement, and she'd lose the flimsy excuse for a bathing suit clinging precariously to her frame.

To her very slender, distractingly feminine frame.

He turned away, annoyed again. "Not right now, son. Later, perhaps."

"But you said you would as soon as you came home again. You *promised!* And you've been home for *hours!*"

"You're right." He sighed, accepting defeat.

"And you told me it's bad to break a promise."

"Right again." He buried a smile. "Okay, you win. Give me ten minutes to clean up and change, and we'll have a quick lesson before breakfast."

Perhaps she'd be gone by then, and they'd have the pool to themselves.

The water lapped around her like warm cream. Very pleasant, very relaxing. *I could make a habit of this,* she thought, stretching luxuriously and breathing deeply of the flower-scented air. *Given enough time and exposure, I might even learn to enjoy it.*

From within the house came the faint clink of dishes and the whispery sound of soft-soled shoes hurrying over marble-tiled floors. She had no idea of the time, but it occurred to her that if the servants were readying breakfast for the family, she should vacate the premises. She had no wish for further contact with Ethan Beaumont. She'd seen enough of him, for one day.

But even as she rolled over and swam sedately toward the steps at the corner of the pool, a child in bright blue swimming trunks came roaring across the terrace, squealing with glee the whole time. And right behind him came Ethan.

"Wait!" he called out.

But the child either didn't hear or chose not to, and with another squeal, shot through the air like a bullet and landed practically on top of her. The relatively calm surface of the water churned in a turbulent froth, smacking her in the face and blinding her. Choking, she lunged for the side of the pool, misjudged the distance, and went under.

To panic when she knew all she had to do was stand up and she'd find herself only waist-deep in water was ridiculous, but that didn't stop her from flailing and thrashing around like a wild thing. The humiliation of that exhibition, though, paled beside the insult of suddenly finding herself being hauled upright by the hair.

Spluttering, she surfaced again and came eyeball to eyeball with Ethan Beaumont. He knelt on the tiled deck, his mouth quivering with suppressed laughter. "Idiot!" he said softly.

"Caveman!" she spluttered. "Do you make a habit of dragging women around by the hair?"

"Only when they're in danger of drowning or otherwise causing themselves grievous bodily harm." Releasing her, he rose smoothly to his feet, and she saw that he'd exchanged the denim shorts for black swimming trunks which showed rather more tanned skin than she felt able to cope with at that moment. "Stay put and I'll give you a lesson on water survival."

"No, thanks," she told him, but she might as well have saved her already tortured breath. He'd turned away and was striding to the other end of the pool, and any inclination she might have had, to escape while she could, faded as she watched him. Tall, broad at the shoulder and narrow at the waist, he moved with the sort of masculine grace few men possessed.

A splashing at her side drew her attention to the child treading water furiously to stay afloat. "That's my papa," he panted, his sweet little face beaming with pride. "He can teach you to swim. He can do everything."

Perhaps not everything, she thought, swinging her gaze back just in time to see Ethan Beaumont dive into the pool so cleanly that he barely caused a ripple, *but I can see why his son might think so. The man is frighteningly competent.*

He surfaced next to her, his hair seal-dark against his skull and water streaming down his torso in sparkling rivulets. ''Lesson number one,'' he said. ''Learn to be comfortable with your face submerged.''

''It'll never happen,'' she said flatly. ''At least, not with me.''

''That's what Adrian said, in the beginning. But he soon changed his mind.'' He looked at her inquiringly. ''Have you met my son?''

''Not formally. I'd hoped to meet him last night, but by the time we'd finished dinner, it was past his bedtime.''

''Then allow me to introduce you now.'' He extended his arm for the child to grasp. ''This is Adrian, who just turned five.''

''Hello, Adrian.'' She smiled at him. He was a beautiful child, black haired like his father and with huge dark brown eyes fringed in long black lashes. ''I'm Anne-Marie.''

He smiled back, but Ethan frowned disapprovingly. ''I prefer that he call you *Mademoiselle.*''

It was on the tip of her tongue to tell him she didn't care what he preferred, but decided it was something better said when they didn't have an audience. So, keeping her smile in place even though doing so made her face ache, she said, ''I should be getting back to my quarters. Solange is surely awake by now, and wondering where I am.''

''No hurry,'' he said, clamping his free hand around her wrist. ''I sent a message for her to join us for breakfast on the terrace. She should be here any moment. We'll make use of the time until she arrives, and start your swimming lesson. Now, to begin—''

''I'm sure you mean well, *Ethan,*'' she said, taking private delight in the way his mouth tightened at the familiarity, "but just as you have your preferences, so do I have mine. And I prefer not to take advantage of your offer, especially not if it means leaving your son to his own devices when he's clearly expecting to spend this time with you."

He released her just long enough to boost Adrian onto the pool deck and murmur something in his ear which sent the boy scooting over to a canopied stall loaded with towels and swimming paraphernalia. Then, turning his attention back to her, he said implacably, "Adrian doesn't mind waiting a few minutes. So, to begin, I'll fit you with a face mask. That way, you'll be able to see under water without discomfort to your eyes."

"I don't want a face mask. I don't want a lesson. How much more plainly do I have to put it?"

"You're afraid."

"Yes, I'm afraid. Is that all right with you?"

"No, it isn't. As long as you're cavorting in pools on my property, I'm responsible for your well-being. I could ensure it by forbidding you to use them, but in this climate they're less a luxury than a necessity. So for your own comfort and my peace of mind, I must insist you allow me to teach you the rudiments of water safety." He paused and surveyed her mockingly. "If a five-year-old can master them, surely a woman your age can at least try to do likewise?"

For a moment, she glared at him without replying, but already the heat was intense and she knew that, as the day progressed and the sun climbed higher in the cloudless sky, it would only get worse. So when it became obvious he wasn't about to accept silence as an answer, she said grudgingly, "Much though I loathe to admit it, it's possible you're right. On all counts."

He selected one of the two masks Adrian had dropped on the side of the pool, declared with irritating superiority, "Of course I am, so let's get on with it," then proceeded to clamp the wretched contraption snugly over her face, and adjust the strap holding it in place. "How does that feel?"

"Fine, I suppose," she said, vibrantly conscious of his touch and the proximity of their near-naked bodies. Although harmless enough on the surface, there was something implicitly intimate about the situation.

"Excellent!" Quickly, he slipped on the other mask, and taking her by both hands, backed away from the steps.

Instantly, the fear grabbed at her. "Don't pull me into deep water!" she begged, resisting him.

"Relax, *Mademoiselle!* All we're going to do is remain perfectly still and look at the bottom of the pool, like so…." He took a breath, lowered his face into the water, blew out a stream of bubbles, then raised his head. "Very simple, very safe, yes?"

"You make it look easy."

"Because it is. Try it and see for yourself."

Cautiously, she followed his instructions and surprised herself. It wasn't nearly as terrifying or alien an experience as she'd expected. The tiles on the bottom of the pool glimmered in the sun-shot blue light. By turning her head slightly, she could see the steps in the corner, a reassuring sight. And when she felt herself running short of air, she simply lifted her face and filled her lungs with a fresh supply.

"I can't believe I'm able to do this!" she said, absurdly pleased with her small accomplishment.

"But you are, and very well, too." Without warning, he tugged her off her feet. "So now we progress to the next level and float."

"Ahh!" She let out a little yelp of fright as, powerless in his hold, she found herself traveling even farther away from the steps.

But he wouldn't let fear get the better of her. "Concentrate," he ordered, his voice low and hypnotic as he towed her effortlessly alongside him. "Remember—lift and breathe, lower and blow."

She did, becoming so engrossed in following his directions that she didn't notice how far they'd traveled until a shadow fell across the water and, looking up, she found herself under the diving board at the deep end of the pool. Again, the familiar panic rose up, and again, before it got the better of her, he tightened his hold and said soothingly, "You're perfectly safe, *Mademoiselle*. I won't let anything happen to you."

"I believe you," she panted, and the amazing thing was, she did. A total stranger had lured her far out of her depth and into dangerous territory, and for some insane reason, she trusted him implicitly. Not for years, not since she was a little girl, had she known such a sense of security, and she rather liked it.

Her voice must have betrayed something of what she was feeling because he pushed up his face mask and, for the first time since they'd met, he smiled. The problem then was not that she'd forget to breathe properly with her face in the water, but that she'd forget to breathe at all. Because his smile transformed him and he became not merely handsome, but truly gorgeous. Flawless in every detail, from his dazzling white and perfect teeth to the brilliant azure of his eyes. And she, fleetingly paralyzed by the moment, could only gaze in spellbound admiration.

Slowly, he disentangled his fingers from hers, as if he were as reluctant to release her as she was to have him let go. "One more thing, and then it's Adrian's turn," he said, giving her slight push. "Swim to the ladder over there, under your own steam." Then, before she could give voice to the protest rising in her throat, he added. "It's either that or make your way back to the shallow end which is five times the distance away."

Did pride give her the courage to do as he asked, or was winning his respect what motivated her? That she hardly knew how to answer the question disturbed her. What he thought of her shouldn't matter. And yet, it did. Rather more than she cared to admit.

Heart pounding, she breast-stroked to the ladder, grasped the lowest rung and pushed off her mask. Then, aware of his gaze focused on every inch of her as she climbed out of the water, she hoisted herself onto the pool deck, resisted the impulse to check that her bikini remained in place, and said, "Thank you for the lesson."

Then, with as much nonchalance as she could muster, she strolled to where Solange waited with Adrian on the bench at the shallow end of the pool. "I thought you'd never get here," she muttered, picking up a towel.

A smile twitched at the corners of Solange's mouth. "I hardly think you missed me."

Anne-Marie waited until Adrian had jumped into his father's waiting arms and was happily splashing his way toward a huge red ball floating on the water, then she said, "Exactly what do you mean by that?"

"Just that you and my future brother-in-law appeared too wrapped up in each other to notice anyone else."

"He insisted on teaching me to use a face mask." She mopped the dripping ends of her hair, then tucked the towel around herself, sarong-style. "And all I can say is, it's a pity no one ever taught him how to take 'No' for an answer. He's very bossy."

"And you're unusually flustered."

Unwilling to debate the truth of that statement, she said, "Never mind me. How are *you*, this morning? You're looking a bit more cheerful than you were last night."

"That's because you're here. I don't feel so alone anymore." She gestured to the terrace. "Breakfast is ready. Shall we go over and sit down?"

Anne-Marie glanced covertly at Ethan who was still in the pool with his son. "Shouldn't we wait for the lord and master to give us permission to eat?"

"He's not an ogre, Anne-Marie! He won't be upset if we help ourselves to coffee. Finish drying off and let's go. I'm never properly awake until—"

"You've had your morning *café au lait*." She laughed, then pulled on her cover-up and slipped her arm through Solange's. "I remember!"

The inflated ball hit Ethan squarely on the shoulder and bounced into the water. "Papa," Adrian called out reproachfully, "you're not paying attention!"

"I know." How could he be expected to, with her laughter floating through the air like music, and the graceful, easy way she moved her scantily-clad body distracting him every other second? But since he could hardly tell his son that, he sniffed conspicuously, boosted the boy onto the pool deck, and said, "I'm thinking about food instead. Jeanne made fruit crêpes for breakfast. I'll race you to the terrace."

The women were chatting animatedly as he approached, and Solange had color in her cheeks, for a change. "You're looking more rested this morning, *ma petite*," he said, dropping a kiss on her head. "Having *Mademoiselle* Barclay here appears to agree with you."

"*Oui.* I am very happy."

"As happy as when you're spending time with Philippe?"

His technique must leave something to be desired because, as usual, she didn't recognize that he was teasing her. "Oh, never that, Ethan!" she said, horrified. "No one can take his place."

"I'm glad to hear it, especially since he phoned this morning to say he'll be home in time for dinner tonight."

Her face lit up—she really was a pretty little thing which, no doubt, was what had first caught Philippe's eye—but she had a fragility about her, and a desire to please at all costs which, combined with a lack of confidence in her own judgment, worried Ethan. This friend, this Anne-Marie Barclay with the long, tanned legs, minuscule bikini, and outspoken manner, didn't strike him as the best influence. The sooner Philippe reappeared and kept Solange occupied, the better.

"So, *Mademoiselle*," he said, taking a seat opposite his guest, "tell me something about yourself."

CHAPTER THREE

"WHAT would you like to know?" Anne-Marie asked pertly, ticked off by his patronizing attitude. Clearly, his expectations of her possible accomplishments hovered around zero.

He shrugged. "As much as you care to tell me. Let's begin with your work. You've designed Solange's wedding trousseau, I understand."

"Yes."

"As a professional, or is this a favor between friends?"

"Both," she said sharply. "I'm a graduate of *Esmode International* in Paris, one of the foremost schools of fashion design in the world."

"Very commendable, I'm sure. And you work—?"

"In Vancouver, on the west coast of Canada."

"I'm aware of where it is, *Mademoiselle*. I've visited your beautiful city a number of times and greatly enjoyed its many attractions. But it hardly struck me as the center of *haute couture*. For which fashion house do you design?"

"My own."

He almost curled his lip in disdain. "I see."

"Do you?" she inquired, matching his condescending tone. "Then you're no doubt aware that my designs have won a number of prestigious awards."

"Anne-Marie worked in the movie industry in Hollywood for a while," Solange cut in, trying to be helpful. "She was even nominated for an Oscar, once."

"Hollywood?" This time, he *did* curl his lip, as if he'd

discovered something disgusting crawling around in the mango-stuffed crêpe the butler placed before him. *"The movie industry?"*

"Yes," Anne-Marie purred, taking a certain vengeful delight in his ill-contained horror. "Theatrical costume has always interested me."

"But you're no longer connected to the entertainment world? You've moved on to a less...flamboyant clientele?"

"Not really. We have a thriving movie industry in Vancouver, too, which is what originally drew me back to my hometown. As a result of the contacts I've made there and in California, I number quite a few well-known stars among my private clients, as well as celebrities from other walks of life."

"And you've designed Solange's wedding dress," he said glumly, rolling his eyes. *"Mon Dieu!"*

"Why does that disturb you, Ethan?" she asked. "I assure you I'm up to the challenge of creating an appropriate wedding ensemble for the bride and her entourage."

He compressed his rather beautiful mouth. "We are a small, close-knit community on Bellefleur. Tradition plays a big part in our lives. A wedding—particularly a Beaumont wedding—is a significant cultural event. My family has certain standards to uphold, certain expectations to meet."

"What a shame," she said blandly. "Where I come from, a wedding's simply a happy event where people who care about the bride and groom come together to celebrate their commitment to one another. And although I don't expect you'll approve, it's also an occasion when the bride gets to call most of the shots. It is, primarily, *her* day."

"How unfortunate for the man who chose her as his bride."

"Why?"

"Because such an attitude shows a distinct lack of consideration for what the groom might prefer—and that does not bode well for harmony in the marriage."

"What a load of rubbish!" she scoffed, ignoring Solange's gasp of petrified horror. "Marriage is a lifelong contract whose success depends on mutual consideration and respect. A wedding, on the other hand, is a one-day affair in which, historically, the bride takes star billing. For a man who professes to set such store by tradition, I'd have thought you'd know that."

"And you're qualified to make that distinction, as well as dictate fashions trends, are you?"

"I've never been married, if that's what you're asking."

"Then you'll forgive me if I take your opinions with a grain of salt."

"Of course I will," she said sunnily. "Just as I'm sure you'll forgive me if I treat yours the same way since, as I understand it, you're divorced—which certainly indicates *you* don't have much of a grasp on how marriage is supposed to work, either."

Only eyes as intensely blue as his could assume such a hard, metallic sheen. "We appear to have strayed from the subject at hand," he said coldly. "Namely, this family's wedding."

"Which you're afraid I'll turn into a tasteless Hollywood spectacle."

He inclined his head in offensively tacit agreement. "I don't mean to insult you."

"Insult me?" Very much aware of Adrian taking in everything without really understanding the subtext of what was being said, she swallowed the temper threatening to get the better of her, and cooed sweetly, "You're downright offensive, Ethan, and on the strength of what? You know next to nothing about me.''

''I know that you're afraid of water.''

He, too, spoke lightly, as if trying to defuse the tension swirling through the air, but she was having none of it. ''I'm not afraid of *you*, though,'' she said. ''Nor do I care what you think of me or my achievements. I'm here to lend moral support to Solange, not win your approval.''

''I applaud your loyalty, but just for the record, *Mademoiselle* Barclay, you're not the only one with Solange's best interests at heart. We all want to see her happy.''

''Then we really don't have anything to disagree about, do we, Ethan? And since I'm calling you by your given name, you may call me Anne-Marie.''

He choked on his coffee at that. ''Thank you, I'm sure,'' he said, when he recovered himself. ''So tell me, *Mademoiselle*, what are your plans for the rest of the day?''

''I'll be working on Solange's wedding gown.''

''Would you care to join us for lunch and perhaps take a tour of the island this afternoon?''

''No, thank you.''

He lifted his brows in faint surprise. Clearly, he wasn't accustomed to being turned down. *Well, he might as well get used to the idea,* she thought, pushing her chair back from the table, *because I've got a feeling he's in for quite a few more upsets before this visit's over.*

Ever the perfect gentleman, he also rose to his feet. ''You're leaving so soon? I hope I'm not the reason. Just because we don't see eye to eye—''

''Don't flatter yourself, Ethan. You have nothing to do with my leaving. As I said a moment ago, I have work to do.''

''Very well. Would you like me to send our in-house seamstress to give you a hand?''

''That's not necessary. I'm perfectly capable of mastering this project on my own.''

For a moment, he chewed on the concept that the world could indeed spin without his directing it, and didn't seem to find the notion very appealing. At length, he said, ''You have everything you need in the way of equipment?''

''Absolutely...except for—''

''Ah!'' He favored her with another smile, a Cheshire-cat kind this time, full of smug satisfaction, as though to say *I knew all this fine independence wouldn't carry you very far.*

''I will need an ironing board.''

''We have staff who take care of ironing.''

''Not with my projects, you don't! I'm the only one who touches them.''

''As you wish.'' He inclined his aristocratic head again, as though conferring enormous favors on an undeserving minion. ''Is there anything else I can supply?''

''Yes,'' she said, spurred to be difficult just for the sake of proving that he wasn't as all-powerful as he liked to believe. ''I could use a worktable—something about eight feet long and at least three feet wide—with a padded muslin top to protect the delicate dress fabrics I'm working with.''

''I'll see to it that one is delivered to your suite immediately,'' he replied, promptly dispelling any illusion she might have entertained that she could play one-upmanship with him and win. ''You do realize, of course, that it's going to leave you rather short of living space?''

''That's not a problem. I'm sure Solange won't mind sharing her sitting room with me, should the occasion arise that I need one.''

"If she does, feel free to relax here at the main house."

I'd rather live in a hovel on the beach than spend a moment more than I have to under your roof! she was tempted to reply but, aware of Solange nervously following the tenor of the conversation, said only, "Thank you. I appreciate the offer."

"You're welcome." He leaned down to ruffle his son's dark hair. "I'll arrange for the worktable to be delivered. Come along, Adrian."

The boy looked hopefully at Solange. "I want to play at Solange's house."

"You'll just be in the way now that *Mademoiselle* Barclay is here. She'll be keeping Solange very busy."

"As long as he doesn't mind my borrowing her for a fitting once in a while, he won't be in the way at all," Anne-Marie said, smiling at the child. "Let him come. It'll give us a chance to get to know one another better."

"Very well." As he passed behind her chair, Ethan laid a surprisingly affectionate hand on Solange's shoulder. "Just phone when you've had enough, *chérie*. Don't let him wear you out."

"He almost sounds as if he cares about you," Anne-Marie muttered, watching Ethan lope gracefully up the steps and disappear inside the villa.

"He does. I already told you, he's very kind and very well-intentioned." Solange covered her mouth to smother a giggle. "But you were deliberately baiting him, Anne-Marie, and succeeding rather well, I might add. I nearly had a heart attack at the way the two of you were going at each other."

"He's the kind of man who brings out the worst in me."

"Is that what you call it?" This time, Solange didn't try to hide her amusement. "From where I sat, it looked more like two people taking refuge in hostility, because they didn't want to admit to the instant attraction between them.''

''That's the most ridiculous thing I ever heard!''

Although her reply held a convincing ring of certainty, Anne-Marie couldn't prevent an annoying shudder of awareness skating over her skin. Ethan Beaumont's penetrating blue gaze *had* unnerved her—more than she was willing to acknowledge. She *was* vibrantly conscious of the physical presence of the man, no matter how much she tried to ignore it.

''I didn't say it made sense,'' Solange replied cheerfully. ''That sort of spontaneous combustion seldom does. But that's no reason to deny it.''

Oh yes, it was! Just because Ethan Beaumont was all smooth, male beauty on the outside didn't mean he wasn't full of flaws on the inside, and she wasn't about to compromise her heart by allowing a purely physical reaction to rule the day!

He heard the laughter long before he reached the guest pavilions: Adrian's high and exuberant, Solange's rippling with unusual delight—and *hers,* breathless, musical, alluring.

Emerging noiselessly from the path, he stood a moment in the filtered shade cast by a giant tibouchina at the edge of the terrace, and saw at once the cause of so much hilarity. A kitten, one of the stable cat's latest litter and not yet as surefooted as it should be, was chasing a balloon tethered to a length of ribbon tied around Adrian's wrist.

The gleeful expression on his son's face sent a stab of pain through Ethan's heart. There'd been too much grief and not nearly enough laughter in the boy's life. Too many nights filled with bad dreams and tears; too many questions left unanswered. Because how did a man explain to a three-year-old that the woman he'd once called "Mommy" had grown tired of the role? Had gone and was never coming back?

Ethan's personal sense of betrayal had long ago faded into indifference. If he thought of his ex-wife at all—and it happened rarely—the most he felt was pity and disgust. But what she'd done to their son left a permanently bitter taste on his tongue. It had been two years since she ran off, and although Adrian no longer asked about her, the damage she'd done had left its mark on the boy.

Certainly, Ethan tried to pick up the slack. Loved enough for two parents. Did everything in his power to create a secure, impregnable world. His shoulders were broad enough to carry the child all day, if need be; his arms strong.

But when the gremlins came and filled the night with terror, he lacked a woman's tender touch, her soft, reassuring voice and sweet, welcoming curves. And seeing how Adrian leaned against the North American visitor and instinctively hid his face against her breasts as the kitten lunged at him, Ethan realized with fresh awareness just how much was missing from his son's life.

"You ought to stay out of the sun, *Mademoiselle*," he said, driven forward less by concern for her welfare than the surge of jealousy which struck out of nowhere and whispered that she had no right trying to supplant him. She was a stranger, a temporary fixture in their lives. She didn't belong and never would. He didn't want her insinuating herself into his boy's affections, just to leave him high and dry when she grew bored with playing nursemaid. "Fair-skinned people like you burn very quickly in this part of the world."

"I used sunscreen," she said offhandedly, nuzzling Adrian's neck.

She'd exchanged the bikini for a yellow sundress held up by shoestring straps. Her arms and feet were bare. As for the parts in between...unwillingly, Ethan noted how the fabric clung to her tiny waist, flared over her narrow hips, and ended halfway down her thighs.

The kitten swatted again at the balloon, missed, and attacked her toes instead. Giggling helplessly, Adrian curled up in her lap and wiggled his toes, too.

"That's enough, Adrian!" Ethan called out, more sharply than he intended. "You're making a nuisance of yourself."

Fending off the kitten, she hugged the boy and stroked the hair from his forehead. "No, he's not. We're having a wonderful time playing, aren't we, Adrian?"

"Yes." He squirmed against her, and wound his arms around her neck.

Almost choking on outrage, Ethan said, "I thought you were here to work, *Mademoiselle*."

"I am," she said, the sweetness in her voice belied by the evil glance she cast him from beneath her lowered lashes. "But since I'm my own boss, I don't need anyone else's permission to take time off for a little fun."

And if he didn't soon put a leash on her tongue, she'd create even more trouble than was already brewing! "That doesn't give you the right to countermand my instructions to my son."

"Good grief!" Rolling her eyes, she released Adrian, gave him a little pat on his behind, and said, "The master calls, sweet pea. Better not keep him waiting. But come back soon, okay?"

"I know how busy you are, Ethan," Solange cut in, eyeing him apprehensively, "and if you'd phoned, I could have brought Adrian home and saved you having to come and get him."

"I was headed down here anyway," he said, wishing she wouldn't tiptoe around him as if she were walking on eggshells all the time. "I wanted to be sure *Mademoiselle* Barclay has everything she needs for her work."

"I do," the other one said, rising languidly to her feet and tugging the skirt of her sundress snugly around her thighs.

He averted his gaze and pretended an interest in the diving board. "The table's satisfactory?"

"Perfectly. Thank you."

"Would you like to see my wedding gown?" Solange asked. "It's truly gorgeous, Ethan."

"He's not interested," her bossy friend informed her. "He's got more important things to do."

Not sure what demon of curiosity provoked him—she herself or merely her work—he said, "Certainly I'm interested! Nothing's more important than pleasing my family, *Mademoiselle*. By all means, show me the dress."

Anne-Marie Barclay stared at him, her mouth set in a delectably stubborn pout, and for a moment, he thought she'd refuse him. After a moment's reflection though, she grudgingly led the way to her villa and waved him inside.

Brushing past her—an unsettling experience, fraught with awareness of her scent and the proximity, again, of her cool, creamy skin—he paused under the covered entrance and stared in disbelief at the sight before him.

Except for the foyer which looked more or less as usual, he barely recognized the place. Gone were the elegant arrangement of furniture, the silk-shaded reading lamps, the bowls of fresh fruit and vases of cut flowers.

The silver candelabra normally gracing the middle of the table in the dining alcove had been banished in favor of her sewing machine, with the iron and ironing board stationed close by.

The main salon was barely recognizable. All the furniture had been pushed against the walls to make room for the worktable, leaving so little floor space that two people couldn't pass one another without body contact—something he'd be wise to avoid where she was concerned, he reminded himself.

"Well, there it is." She indicated some sort of dummy figure in the corner, with the wedding gown draped over it. "Perfectly respectable, as you can see."

"I never doubted that for a moment."

"Oh, please!" she exclaimed, putting the length of the table between them in order to make some small adjustment to the dress. "You anticipated nothing of the sort. The only reason you professed an interest in seeing my work was to prove conclusively how totally ill-equipped I am to handle the task I've undertaken."

"Possibly." He inched his way down the other side of the table and circled the garment, taking note of the myriad pearl-headed pins holding the cobweb-fine fabric in place. Even he, ignorant though he was when it came to the finer points of women's fashions, could appreciate the clean, clever lines of the bodice and the artful drape of the skirt. "But if so, my reservations were clearly misplaced, although I confess I expected the dress would be more or less finished by now. As it is, you appear to have quite a bit of work still to do."

"It just needs to be put together," she said, as if such a major feat of engineering was a mere trifle to a person of her expertise. "I wanted to be sure of a perfect fit before any permanent stitching went into place. This fabric's too delicate to tolerate much in the way of alterations."

"So you did the preliminary work ahead of time on the dummy? How'd you manage to fit it into a suitcase?"

"I didn't," she answered saucily. "I pack my equipment in a small cabin trunk and although it's roomy enough for most things, try as I might, I couldn't squeeze myself inside. But if you're referring to the dress form, it comes apart and actually takes up very little space.''

Unable to repress a smile, he said dryly, ''We appear to have difficulty communicating, *Mademoiselle*.''

''Oh, I don't think so,'' she replied, around a mouthful of pins. ''I think we understand one another perfectly. Neither of us is the least bit impressed with the other. If it were up to you, I'd be on my way home by now.''

The glance she flung at him dared him to deny it, nor was he inclined to do so. ''Yes, you would,'' he admitted. ''But since that's clearly not about to happen, the question now becomes, what can we do to reverse such an unfortunate state of affairs?''

She removed the pins from her mouth and poked them into a fat pink cushion designed for the purpose. ''You mean to say, you're not even going to pretend to deny one exists?''

''Certainly not. I have good reason to mistrust you, although I fail to see why you should be so antagonistic toward me.''

Her mouth fell open, whether in mock surprise or because she truly was amazed by what she obviously interpreted as unabashed arrogance on his part. But much though he'd have preferred to take advantage of her discomposure and emerge the winner in their little contest of wills, he found to his chagrin that his attention was drawn to how deliciously pink and ripe her lips were. Would they taste as sweet, he wondered.

She planted her fists on her hips. ''What possible reason do you have to mistrust me?''

''It's not something I'm prepared to discuss at present,'' he said, glancing meaningfully to where Adrian was playing with his kitten under the covered walkway. "More to the point, why are you so hostile?"

"That's easily answered," she said bluntly. "You're not my type. I've never cared for overbearing men. Not that either issue matters one iota since I'm here for only a few weeks and, once the wedding's over, we'll never have to see each other again."

"I disagree. Even a day can seem like a very long time when two people find themselves frequently thrown into one another's company. And make no mistake about it, *Mademoiselle*. We *will* be spending a great deal of time together in the coming weeks."

"Why? We're not the couple getting married."

"Indeed not, and for that I'm deeply and enduringly grateful," he said, taking private pleasure in the flush which ran under her skin at his response. "But weddings, at least Beaumont weddings, amount to a bit more than a church ceremony and a reception. As best man, it's my duty to escort the maid of honor to the various social events taking place between now and the big day itself. That being so, surely you agree we need to arrive at some sort of truce?"

"I'm perfectly capable of looking after myself. So thank you anyway, but no thank you, Ethan. I neither want nor need you to act as my chaperon."

A third voice, young and filled with confusion, brought them swinging around to find Adrian standing just inside the foyer. "Don't you like my papa, Anne-Marie?"

"Oh, sweetheart...!" Gray eyes wide with distress, she hurried around the worktable and dropping to her knees, cupped his face in her hands. "I didn't say I didn't like him."

Not in so many words, perhaps! Annoyed as much with himself as with her, for forgetting how easily sound traveled through the open shutters of the building, Ethan joined her and placed his hand on his son's shoulder. "I thought I told you to stay with Solange, *mon petit?*"

"She went inside to answer her phone," he said, his gaze fixed adoringly on the face of his new friend. "She was gone a long time, and the kitten ran off, so I came to find you."

"You did the right thing," the Barclay woman murmured soothingly. "It was very rude of us to leave you alone, but your father and I are finished our conversation now, so why don't you and I play another game?"

"No," Ethan said, taking Adrian's hand firmly in his. "I already made it clear he won't be staying."

"And I made it clear he's no trouble."

But you are, he thought. *You're nothing but trouble, and I intend to put a stop to it before you cause irreparable damage to my boy.* "No," he said again, more forcefully this time. "He comes with me. You can't possibly attend to your work and keep an eye on him at the same time."

"I'm a woman," she retorted, as if he hadn't already noticed. "I can multitask."

"I'm a father, and I don't care to have my son left to his own devices around a swimming pool, especially not with someone who doesn't have the first clue about water rescue or life-saving techniques."

"Oh, rats!" She made a comical face and rubbed her nose against Adrian's, thereby reducing him to another fit of giggles. "Father's right again, but never mind, sweet pea. We'll have lots of other chances to play."

Not if he had anything to say in the matter, as she'd discover soon enough, Ethan thought grimly, steering Adrian outside just as Solange emerged from her quarters.

"There's someone waiting to see you in your office,"

she told him. "A Señor Gonzales from Caracas. Something to do with the oil operations, I understand."

"I wasn't expecting him until tomorrow." He pointed Adrian toward the path leading uphill. "Guess we'd better head home, *mon petit.*"

"Yes, do," Anne-Marie Barclay said, with unflattering enthusiasm. "There's certainly nothing to keep you here."

"Not at this moment, perhaps," he said, determined to have the last word, "but I'll be back. And when I return, it'll be to establish a few ground rules. Because you'll surely concur that we need to arrive at some sort of harmonious understanding of who's calling the shots around here."

"You haven't left me in much doubt about that."

"I'd like to think not. But you don't strike me as someone who concedes defeat easily."

She lifted one shoulder in a delicate but decidedly defiant shrug.

"Precisely," he said. "So for the good of everyone, but most especially my boy, you and I will arrive at a mutually acceptable agreement which will preclude any further clashing of wills. Because I will not subject him to any more such displays, nor will I allow our incompatibility to turn my brother's pre-wedding festivities into a battle zone."

CHAPTER FOUR

ANNE-MARIE didn't see him again until that evening when, unlike the day before, dinner was a formal affair involving the whole family.

"You look lovely," Solange told her, as they made their way through the gardens to the Sunset Gazebo for the cocktail hour. "Is that outfit one of your own creations?"

"Of course. I make all my own clothes."

"Well, seeing you tonight ought to put an end to any doubts Ethan still has about your talent. He's sure to be impressed."

"I didn't dress to please him," she said sharply, but it wasn't true. She'd deliberately chosen the violet chiffon dress for its dramatic neckline which left one shoulder bare, and for the way it lent her gray eyes a smoky purple depth at the same time that it emphasized her ivory-toned skin.

I'll knock his socks off! she'd vowed defiantly, glaring at herself in the mirror as she secured her hair in a smooth coil on the crown of her head, and swept a trace of lavender shadow over her eyelids. *Before this evening's over, there'll be no doubt in anyone's mind about which of us knows the most about good taste!*

But when they finally came face-to-face, she was the one left speechless. If Ethan stripped to the waist in the cool shade of morning was spectacular, Ethan in white dinner jacket and black tie, with the setting sun turning his skin to glowing bronze, was breathtaking.

"I'm delighted you decided to join us," he said, as if

there was even a remote possibility that *anyone* would have the nerve to refuse a Beaumont invitation. "Allow me to introduce my aunt and uncle, Josephine and Louis Duclos. This," he said, drawing her toward the couple waiting to the rear, "is Solange's friend, *Mademoiselle* Anne-Marie Barclay."

"Enchanté, Mademoiselle," Louis Duclos murmured, kissing her hand with old-world gallantry. "Welcome to Bellefleur."

"Indeed," his wife said, with a cool smile, and tapped him on the shoulder. "That's enough, Louis! Release *Mademoiselle* Barclay's hand, if you please, before you swallow it whole, and allow her to make my acquaintance. *Mademoiselle,* you may sit with me under the canopy."

Issuing orders under the guise of invitations must be a Beaumont family trait, Anne-Marie decided, accepting the proffered seat. And with the exception of her eyes, which were the same dark brown as Adrian's, Josephine's striking resemblance to Ethan marked her as a Beaumont born and bred.

"Tell me about yourself," she commanded, her gaze raking over Anne-Marie with daunting candor. "I know nothing about you except that you and Solange are old friends. How did that come about, given that she is French and you're Canadian? Were your parents also members of the diplomatic corps?"

"No. My parents died in a boating accident when I was eight."

Josephine's gaze softened marginally. "I'm sorry. That was a grievous loss for such a young child to endure. Were you left completely alone?"

"Not quite. My mother had a brother who became my guardian. But he was a bachelor in his early twenties. He hadn't the first idea how to cope with a little girl who cried every night for her mother and father. So he sent me away to boarding school where I'd at least be with other children my own age, and eventually to the Swiss finishing school where Solange and I met.''

''And became friends because you had so much in common. Not that she was orphaned, of course, but she might as well have been since her parents so seldom showed interest in her.''

''They didn't really abandon me, *Tante* Josephine,'' Solange said, leaping to their defense just as she always had, no matter how often they forgot her birthday or canceled plans to meet her during school vacations. ''It was just that my father's work in the Consulate was very demanding and involved a great deal of travel. The only reason I spent so much time in boarding school was that he and my mother wanted to maintain some sort of continuity in my education. But they always made sure I attended the *very best* schools.''

''Rationalize it any way you like,'' Josephine replied, ''but the bottom line is, they farmed you out to an institution and left someone else to bring you up while they partied their way through Europe. You're just too nice a child to speak as plainly as I do.''

''I met Solange's parents on several occasions, and they always struck me as very caring people,'' Anne-Marie said, knowing how devastating Solange would find such blunt criticism.

''I'm sure they were, and are,'' Josephine Duclos replied. ''They care a great deal about their own pleasures.''

''They were always extremely kind to me.''

''I'm not saying they were deliberately cruel, young woman.'' Josephine spared Ethan a telling glance. ''Merely self-involved to the exclusion of those around them, like someone else we once knew.''

"Let's not air our dirty linen all at once," he said mildly. "*Mademoiselle* Barclay's opinion of us is already tarnished enough."

"I don't know why you'd assume that," Anne-Marie replied, accepting a glass of champagne from Louis Duclos. "Adrian is adorable."

"But I'm not." Although his tone remained cheerfully uncaring, Ethan's smile held more than a touch of irony and caused a minor upheaval in Anne-Marie. Even when he wasn't *trying* to be charming, she found him attractive, so what sort of fool did that make her?

"No," she said, striving to match his insouciance. "You're thoroughly obnoxious!"

At that, Solange visibly cringed but, surprisingly, Josephine let out a squawk of laughter. "I think you've met your match, Ethan," she crowed. "And as for you, child...." She tapped Anne-Marie on the arm. "I do believe I might like you!"

"From which you'll no doubt gather that my aunt doesn't confer approval on too many people," Ethan said dryly. "Would you care for more champagne?"

"Stop trying to make her tipsy. I'm not yet finished quizzing her." Brown eyes snapping with lively curiosity, Josephine turned back to Anne-Marie. "What else about you is interesting, child, beside the fact that you're refreshingly outspoken?"

"Very little. My work keeps me too busy to pursue much in the way of hobbies."

"I'm not talking about what you *do!* It's who you are inside that I want to hear about—your thoughts and opinions. How, for example, do you feel about Solange marrying a Beaumont?"

Dusk was descending rapidly. Already, the shot-silk blue of the sea had deepened to rich plum. But the squat pillar candles encircling a bouquet of scarlet hibiscus on the table threw out enough light for Anne-Marie to be vividly aware of Ethan's gaze sliding from her face to her bare shoulder, dipping slowly all the way to her ankles, then returning to dwell on her face as if he were trying to penetrate her mind and discern her most private thoughts.

He made her wish she'd worn something a little more conservative. Something that didn't reveal quite so much of her. She wanted to hug her arms over her breasts, smooth away the gooseflesh suddenly pebbling her skin. Turn away from that probing regard.

Instead, she found herself hypnotized by it…by him. His hair, dark as night, lay smooth against his skull. Except for his eyes which, even in the fading light, gleamed blue as lapis lazuli, he was a study in tones of sepia, black and white. He lifted his glass in that negligently graceful way with which he appeared to do most things, his hand and wrist tawny against the snowy cuff of his shirt. He blinked slowly, and the charcoal shadow of his lashes flickered over the polished bronze of his cheekbones.

His mouth lifted in a slow smile. "We're all waiting to hear your answer, *Mademoiselle*," he said softly. "Do you think Solange is insane to throw in her lot with a family such as ours?"

"I hope she isn't," she said forthrightly. "I hope Philippe lives up to her expectations."

"But you have doubts that he will?"

She hesitated, hating how he was putting her on the spot, and wishing he hadn't so accurately pinpointed the reservations she'd kept from Solange. The Philippe she remembered was charming and attentive, but he didn't possess a fraction of his brother's strength of character. Solange was emotionally fragile, though. She needed a strong man by her side.

"I haven't seen Philippe in almost eight years," Anne-Marie said, choosing her words with care. "I expect he's changed, so I prefer to withhold comment until we become reacquainted."

Ethan, though, wasn't about to let her off the hook so easily. "Changed from what?" he persisted.

"From the way he used to be, of course—a boy barely out of his teens, playing at being a man of the world. I expect he's grown up somewhat in the time since."

"Don't hold your breath," Josephine Duclos muttered. "Louis, hand me my wrap and escort me back to the house. My stomach tells me it's time I ate."

Even as she spoke, the telephone beside Ethan rang. Lifting it, he strolled to the edge of the gazebo and carried on a brief, low-voiced conversation before turning back to announce, "Your stomach is right on time as usual, *ma tante*. And you, Solange, will be happy to know Philippe arrived home half an hour ago, and will be joining us for dinner."

"He's here already? I wasn't expecting him until much later." She sprang to her feet, her face illuminated with joy. "Will you excuse me if I run ahead?"

"Sure," he said. "Go welcome him back."

She raced off, light-footed as a gazelle, and since Josephine and Louis also had already started back, Anne-Marie was left with no choice but to walk with Ethan.

"So," he said, cupping her elbow in a firm, warm grasp which made it clear he wasn't about to let her wriggle free from his hold or his questions, "now that we're alone at last, tell me exactly what you really think about this marriage between your best friend and my half brother."

"I have mixed feelings, Ethan. Philippe struck me in the past as being very likable but rather spoiled. If he hasn't matured, I'd worry about how ready he is for something as permanent as marriage. On the other hand, I never thought his relationship with Solange would last more than one summer. I take it as a very good sign that it's survived nearly ten years.''

''There have been other women in between, you know.''

''And Solange has dated other men. Yet, in the end, no one could come between her and Philippe. They always found their way back to one another.''

''Does she know how you feel—that you're not sure she's made the wisest choice?''

''No. Solange's confidence is easily crushed and I wouldn't dream of saying anything which might undermine her at this stage of the game. If she'd asked me six months ago, I might have been more candid.''

''It strikes me as strange that, for such good friends, you don't confide in one another more readily. I'd have thought you'd be the first person she'd tell when she became engaged.''

''I'm the person she turns to when things go wrong, Ethan. When life's treating her well, the people she shares her happiness with are her parents, because she knows they don't have either the time or the inclination to involve themselves in her troubles. The only news they're interested in hearing is the good news.''

''So my aunt's observations weren't far off the mark?''

''Sadly not.''

''It makes me wonder why some people bother having children in the first place,'' he said, the note of savagery underlying his tone echoed in his almost bruising grip on her elbow.

''Do *you* have any regrets about fathering Adrian?''

''Good God, no! What sort of question is that?''

''One prompted by the fact that you're practically pulverizing my bones!'' Wincing, she extracted herself from his hold. "To some men, a child is a sort of status symbol, a mark of their masculinity, if you like.''

"And to some women, a child is a toy to be cast aside when they grow tired of playing with it!''

"Are we talking about your ex-wife now?''

"Yes, though I can't imagine how she merits being included in the conversation. She was, if you'll forgive my speaking plainly, a living bitch, and undeserving of a son like Adrian.''

"Abandoning a child is completely contrary to a woman's natural instincts. I think she must have been desperately unhappy to resort to such action.''

"Are you suggesting I'm the one who drove her away?''

"I'm not suggesting anything, merely expressing an opinion I believe in. Normally, it goes against the grain for a mother to abandon her young.''

"There was nothing 'normal' about Lisa! The pity of it is, I didn't recognize the fact sooner. If I had, I could saved everyone, particularly my son, a lot of heartache.''

And what about your pain, Ethan? she wondered, hearing the ragged edge in his voice. *Does it still eat at you when you wake up alone in the night? Is Adrian the only one who misses her?* "If she were to ask to come back, would you let her?''

They had emerged from the path into a clearing swathed in moonlight. The drugging scent of flowers filled the still air but not a sound disturbed the silence—except for his uneven breathing. "Yes,'' he said from between clenched teeth, and it was as if his reply had been torn from his very heart and left him mortally wounded. "Yes, I would let her. How could I not?''

She shouldn't have cared. But his anguish flowed out and entrapped her like a living thing, filling her with an inexplicable, illogical sense of having been robbed. Yet how could that be, when she had nothing to lose in the first place?

When they arrived at the house, they found Josephine and Louis admiring an urn full of gardenias at one end of the dining room verandah, and Philippe and Solange at the other, locked in the kind of uninhibited public embrace which was their habit.

Either his annoyance showed on his face, or else he made an involuntary sound of disapproval because, as they approached, Anne-Marie flung him a scornful glance and said quietly, "What's the matter, Ethan? Jealous?"

"Not in the least," he muttered. "But there's a time and place for everything."

"Not in their case. You've made sure of that by keeping Solange and Philippe apart as much as possible, so who can blame them for making the most of whatever opportunity presents itself?"

"Not you, apparently," he said dourly. "Should I take that to mean you exercise no restraint in your own…affairs?"

"You make 'affairs' sound like a dirty word, Ethan, as if you think men line up around the block, eager to sample whatever sexual favors I choose to bestow."

As though drawn by a powerful magnetic force, his gaze lingered a moment on the graceful sweep of fabric draping itself from her shoulder and across the swell of her breasts to her tiny waist. "I could hardly blame them, if they did."

A delicate peach blush ran over her face. "I'm not sure whether I should be flattered or insulted by that remark."

He was spared having to answer by Philippe who, having finally noticed them, crossed to where they stood and swept Anne-Marie into a hug which struck Ethan as being considerably more enthusiastic than the occasion called for.

"I swear, if I weren't marrying Solange, I'd propose to you, Anne-Marie!" he said. "How come no other man's got my good sense?"

Hearing him, Josephine said tartly, "Perhaps Anne-Marie's the one with sense. Put her down, you fool, and let your brother lead her into dinner before I faint from weakness! What took you so long to get here, Ethan?"

"We were talking and time got away from us."

"Talking about what?" Never one to be fobbed off with half-truths, Josephine stared at him, beady-eyed.

"Children, and how best to deal with them," he replied, trying to ignore the uneasiness which assailed him at the expression on Solange's face as she watched his brother. Did Philippe have any inkling of the depth of her adoration? Did he *deserve* it?

Ushering them all into the dining room, Ethan indicated that Anne-Marie should take her place to the right of where he sat, at the head of the table. She slid onto the chair in one easy, graceful movement, with her dress rippling down her body to swirl in waves around her ankles, thereby drawing his unwilling attention to the physical attributes of the woman wearing it.

The candelabra suspended from the ceiling awoke glimmers of palest wheat in her blond hair and painted fetching shadows on her face. Over the course of the day, she'd picked up a touch of sun—just enough to gild her creamy skin with honey.

She sat close enough that, without it appearing deliberate, he could have nudged her knee with his. Touched her sandaled foot in private intimacy. Had he wished, he could have reached over and covered her hand. Fingered the thin gold chain at her narrow wrist, or the diamond studs winking fire and ice at her ears.

And, shockingly, he did wish—for all those things. Which made him, for once, very glad of his aunt's insatiable interest in other people's lives. It spared him having to make polite conversation with a woman he found altogether more distracting than she had any right to be.

"How old are you, child?" Josephine inquired, over hot papaya-orange soup.

"Twenty-eight."

"And never married?"

"No." She smiled, seeming not at all put out by such a personal line of questions. "I haven't had the time. Or perhaps it's just that I haven't yet met the right man."

"But you have no objection to marriage as such?"

She thought about that for a moment, tipping her head to one side and lowering her lashes so that they lay like miniature fans against her cheeks. Finally, she said, "No. Eventually, I would like a husband and children, and the trappings that go with them."

"By 'trappings,' do you mean money?"

"Good grief, no! I've already got plenty of that."

"Social status, then?" his aunt persisted.

"I consider I have that, too." She cast an amused glance at Ethan. "Although not everyone around this table might agree with me."

"Oh, never mind Ethan," Josephine chortled. "He's the kind of man who, once he makes up his mind about something, there's no moving him. But that's not to say he's always right."

"If I might be allowed to say something in my own defense, I haven't reached any hard and fast conclusions about you, *Mademoiselle*," he said mildly.

"Certainly you have," she retorted. "You've pegged

me as brash, flashy and uncouth when, in fact, I'm guilty only of being brash.''

''Don't put words in my mouth. And don't presume to read my mind.''

Josephine flapped her hand imperiously. ''Ignore him, Anne-Marie. Instead, tell me more about these trappings you're so anxious to acquire.''

''They're not material, if that's what you're wondering,'' she said. ''I want things money can't buy—traditions, I suppose you'd call them, like taking my child to choose his own pumpkin for Halloween, or helping him trim the tree at Christmas, then drinking hot chocolate and singing carols with him, afterward. If I had a daughter, I'd want to sew pretty party dresses for her, and bake special cakes for her birthdays.''

''Because they're the things which were taken away from you at much too early an age. Yes, I can see why they'd be important to you now.'' Josephine nodded sympathetically. ''Would you like to have more than one child?''

''Oh, definitely! Heaven forbid they'd suffer the same loss I did, but at least if it should happen, they'd have each other. In my experience, an only child is too often a lonely child.''

''It doesn't have to be,'' Ethan said defensively.

''No, of course not.'' She shrugged. ''It all depends on the circumstances.''

''And yours were particularly tragic.'' His aunt paused long enough to sample her soup, then started in on another barrage of questions. ''You've worked very hard to make a name for yourself in the world of fashion, my dear. Do you see yourself being able to give up your career in order to raise a family?''

''Not permanently, perhaps, but certainly over the short

haul. I consider motherhood to be a very worthwhile career in itself and deserving of the best a woman can bring to it.''

''*Eh bien,* isn't it fortunate that you're going to be here for several weeks!'' Josephine glanced at Ethan meaningfully. ''And what a pity we didn't meet you seven years ago.''

''For someone who claimed she was starving, you're doing a lot more talking than you are eating,'' he said, knowing full well where his aunt's remarks were leading. She'd never liked Lisa, and had made it her mission in life to fix him up with someone more suitable.

You're my firstborn nephew and my favorite, she'd often told him. *I need to know you're with someone who truly deserves you, before I die.*

''I'm merely being sociable,'' she said now. ''Tell me, Anne-Marie, how do you like this room?''

''Very much. The detailed flower painting on the walls is exquisite. *Trompe l'oeil,* isn't it?''

''Quite right, child, and how delightful that you're cultured enough to recognize it,'' Josephine replied, too transparently pleased at discovering her newfound protégée's latest virtue to recognize her remark came across as insultingly condescending.

''I saw many fine examples of the same in the chateaux I visited when I lived in France,'' Anne-Marie said, further enhancing her image with his aunt. ''In fact, I followed a similar technique with some of my textile designs during my studies.''

''And won a gold medal for them, too,'' Solange said, managing to tear her attention away from Philippe long enough to contribute something to the conversation.

''Did you indeed?'' Josephine smiled, as satisfied as a cat who'd just devoured a bowl of cream, and Ethan privately admitted he was rather impressed himself. Perhaps there was more depth to Anne-Marie Barclay than he'd originally thought.

Still, he was relieved when the butler, Morton, appeared to direct the serving of the second course and Josephine, recognizing her favorite heart of palm salad, turned her attention to her plate.

Leaning toward Anne-Marie, Ethan said in an undertone, "I hope you didn't find my aunt's comments offensive. She means well, but her interest sometimes takes on the tone of an inquisition, and I apologize if it made you uncomfortable."

"It didn't," she replied. "I appreciate her being so direct and I envy you her devotion."

"If you're sincerely interested in the decor of this room, I'll be glad to give you a tour of the house someday when you have an hour to spare."

"That would be very nice."

Would it, or was she merely being polite? he wondered. Was she really as serenely composed as she appeared, or was it more a case of her having perfected the act of appearing so?

As the meal progressed, he found himself observing her. Watching for a hint of what really lay behind her lovely smile. Listening to the musical lilt of her laughter, the slightly husky timbre of her voice. And when, after coffee and cognac, the other four excused themselves and left him alone with her, he heard himself offering to escort her back to her villa with an eagerness which made him wonder if she'd somehow bewitched him.

He'd probably live to regret it, but the prospect of delving below her surface and discovering the real person underneath struck him suddenly as too appealing an undertaking to ignore.

CHAPTER FIVE

"THIS really isn't necessary," Anne-Marie said, as he ushered her past the pillared entrance to the room and out through a side door to the paved terrace. Just when the other four members of the party had drifted off until only the two of them remained lingering over coffee, escaped her, but she did know the prospect of being alone in the deserted gardens with Ethan filled her with peculiar trepidation. "I assure you I can make my own way back."

His laugh flowed over her, low and oddly intoxicating in the warm night. "I somehow doubt that, since you couldn't even find your way here in broad daylight. And the path is steep in places. It wouldn't do to have you fall and hurt yourself. Solange would never forgive me. In any case, I could use a breath of fresh air, and it'll give us a chance to get to know one another better."

"Better? How about 'differently'?" she said.

"I'm not sure I know what you mean."

"Then let me speak bluntly. Your opinion of me underwent a subtle change over dinner and I'm curious to know why. Was it my informed appreciation of the decor in your dining room and the fact that I didn't try to steal the family silver that persuaded you to temper your animosity toward me, or did it take your aunt's stamp of approval to soften your attitude?"

"Have I been such an ogre?" he said lightly. "If so, I apologize."

"That doesn't answer my question."

"Then perhaps this will. Not for a moment did I think

64

you'd steal the family silver, Anne-Marie, nor was your intelligence ever in question. As for my aunt...." Again, his laughter caused an inexplicable sensation of pleasure to ripple over her skin. "I'm so used to Josephine putting her two bits' worth into the conversation every other minute that I barely notice it anymore."

Putting her two bits' worth into the conversation... The American idiom struck an incongruous note, coming as it did from a man who appeared to have little respect for anything remotely American. "You speak with a slight accent," she said, "yet your English is very colloquial."

"French was my mother tongue, but I spent several years studying at Harvard."

"So not everything from my neck of the woods is necessarily bad?"

"Not necessarily, no." She heard the smile in his voice. "I have a number of friends and many business acquaintances in the U.S. But before you accuse me of misleading you, you should know I'm also fluent in Spanish and Portuguese, and have contacts throughout South America, too."

"Then you're one up on me. I speak only French and Italian."

"That would matter only if we were in competition with each other, but since we're not, let's try to put aside our differences and get along, for Solange's sake." He took her hand, tucked it in the crook of his arm, and led her down a gravel path on the far side of the pool, different from the one by which he'd brought her to the mansion earlier. "It's pleasant out here, don't you think?"

"Pleasant" hardly began to describe it. The night was full of stars, some winking down from the heavens, and some gazing up from the ground—exotic lilies, and other flowers she didn't recognize, which looked ghostly pale and almost insubstantial by moonlight, yet were heavy with a scent redolent of earthy passions. It was an enchanted scene, so magical she thought she heard music drifting on the quiet air, and stopped to listen. Yes, there it was: something old-fashioned and rather haunting, in three-quarter time.

"*Deep In My Heart*," Ethan said, pausing too, and she reared back, for a moment startled into thinking he was speaking to her. But then he continued, "It's the refrain from *The Student Prince*, my aunt's favorite operetta. She and my uncle dance to it almost every night. It has great sentimental value for them. He proposed to her the night he took her to see the musical revival on Broadway, over fifty years ago."

"And they still honor the tradition today?" It was such an unexpected story, and one so touchingly reminiscent of the way her own parents had behaved toward one another, that Anne-Marie turned away, embarrassed by the sudden tears stinging her eyes. "That's the way marriages ought to be."

"But seldom are." He thrust a handkerchief at her. "Here. I believe you need this."

"I don't know why I should," she said, feeling like a fool.

"You were caught by surprise. You didn't think there'd be much room for passion or tenderness in a relationship where the wife appears to wear the pants."

"Well, your uncle does seem a little henpecked," she said, smiling again at the odd blending of formality and slang in his speech.

He clasped her hand again, and didn't let go. "On the surface, perhaps, but he's the steel in the backbone of their marriage, which just goes to show how wrong first impressions can be, Anne-Marie, and is a lesson to both of us not to leap to unfounded conclusions. Louis is the light of my aunt's life, and she of his.''

Anne-Marie, he'd called her, and the way he'd said it rendered it so intimate that a flush ran over her.

''That's the way I remember my parents being,'' she said, projecting a calm she was far from feeling. ''I've often thought it was as well they died together because I can't imagine how one would have survived without the other. They needed each other the way other people need oxygen.''

The path opened into a clearing just then, with a lily pond in the middle spanned by a small stone bridge. Leading her toward it, he said, ''But you had needs, too, and I'm beginning to think they've been left neglected too long.''

The moon shone full and bright, splashing the surrounding jungle with silver and flinging long, deep shadows across the surface of the water. A night creature let out a sleepy squawk which somehow intensified the utter stillness of the setting.

''Needs?''

''Yes,'' he said—a simple enough answer and, on the surface at least, not without merit, because the feeling of belonging, of being connected to another person in the most vital way possible, had been missing from her life from the day she'd learned about her parents' death.

She'd searched for it without success in every relationship which had come her way since, but never in her wildest imaginings had she thought she'd find it with a man she'd met little more than twenty-four hours earlier. Yet, all at once, there it was, so tangible she could almost reach out and touch it.

''Why didn't you tell me the reason you're so afraid of the water?'' he said. ''If I'd known your parents drowned

when you were just a child, I'd have been more understanding.''

''Would you?'' she stammered.

''Yes,'' he said again, standing so close that his answer
this time feathered over her lips.

How had it come about, she wondered, dazed, that in
the space of a second, her association with Ethan
Beaumont had shifted to assume a totally different dimen-
sion? At what precise moment had they suddenly ceased
being wary host and defensive guest, and become instead
a man and a woman helplessly drawn to one another by
forces beyond their control?

She had no answer. She knew only that it had happened,
and a breathless, reckless expectation seized her. Without
thought for the consequences, she lifted her face and drank
in the essence of the blossom-scented night. Of him and
the pure masculine magnetism he radiated. She closed her
eyes and waited…waited….

Seconds ticked by, marked only by the urgent thud of
her heart. And then, when she thought she'd been mistaken
after all and nothing had changed between them, he said
raggedly, ''Am I supposed to kiss you now, Anne-Marie?''

She'd have been humiliated beyond endurance if she
hadn't detected the torment behind his remark and realized
the reason for it. But the battle he was fighting—and losing—so closely paralleled her own emotional turmoil that
she found the courage to whisper, ''How about a little
truth, for a change, Ethan? How about 'I *want* to kiss you,
Anne-Marie'?''

''No,'' he muttered. But his hands betrayed him and slid
through her hair, working at the pins holding it up until it
fell loose around her shoulders. ''No,'' he said again, almost savagely. ''It'll never happen.''

''Why not?''

''Because,'' he said, ''it would be a mistake.''

But either he didn't really believe what he was saying, or he, too, was at the mercy of impulses beyond his control, because he dipped his head lower...lower...until it blotted out the moon peeping over his shoulder, and his breath taunted her senses with the memory of the pale gold wine he'd drunk at dinner.

And finally, when she was trembling all over with anticipation, his lips searched out hers. Unable to help herself, she rose to meet him, felt his arms lock around her, and was lost.

His kiss was so much more than a meeting of mouths. It was an introduction to paradise; a promise of something beyond earthly comprehension. Its imprint scorched her soul and left her melting against him.

He awoke every female instinct she possessed and set it free. He reduced every other kiss she'd ever known to ashes; every other man to a featureless shadow.

His mouth lingered, explored, discovered, persuaded. At his instigation, her lips parted to allow her tongue to engage in shameless, erotic intimacy with his. He tasted divine and the more she sampled, the more she craved. The more he demanded, the more she gave.

At length, inevitably, he broke all contact and stepped back to examine her from hooded, unreadable eyes. ''I was right,'' he said hoarsely. ''That was a big mistake.''

''But not necessarily fatal, surely?'' she said, trying not to whimper with disappointment. ''Sometimes, people can learn a great deal from their mistakes.''

''Yes, but that was a lesson I could do without. It taught me nothing I want to know.''

It taught me things I never want to forget, she longed to tell him, but he was in no mood to listen. The warmth he'd briefly lavished on her was gone and he was once again the cool, unwilling host under obligation to a guest not of his choosing.

"Come," he said, gesturing for her to precede him across the bridge. "Your suite is only a few yards farther on."

A moment later, the flickering yellow flames of the tiki lamps bordering the guest pavilions' terrace appeared. The maid had left a small lamp burning in Anne-Marie's foyer, but the adjoining villa was in complete darkness. Just as well. She was in no shape to face Solange.

"You'll be all right now?" he asked.

"Perfectly, thank you."

"Then I'll say good night. I hope you sleep well."

Fat chance, Ethan! "I'm sure I'll sleep like a baby," she replied and, still shaken, went inside and leaned against the wall beside the filigree ironwork at the window of her bedroom, listening.

Over the still-thudding extravaganza of her heart, she heard his footsteps crunch over the gravel and fade away, and wondered how she'd ever face him again without blushing. Because she knew that if he'd asked, she'd have let him stay and would have spent the night in his arms. But worse by far was that she was afraid he knew it, too.

Over the next several days, she avoided him altogether by concentrating on putting together the wedding party's outfits and using that as an excuse to keep away from the main house. She established a routine of working during the early mornings and cool evenings, and spending the stifling midday hours either by, or in, the pool outside her door.

Although by no means ready to tackle anything too ambitious, she found that, with daily practice, she gained a new measure of confidence in the water and took real pleasure in finally being able to swim the forty foot length of the pool without panicking. The sun turned her skin a delicate honey color and lent streaks of shimmering highlights to her already blond hair.

She arranged for her meals to be sent down from the main house. Three times daily, one of the servants would arrive in a small golf cart, with a covered tray—fruit, hot sweet rolls and coffee for breakfast, a salad with more fruit for lunch, and for dinner, whatever the family was having. It was always immaculately prepared, always delicious.

Adrian came to visit most afternoons. His nanny dropped him off about half past two, and picked him up again around four. During their time together, he'd climb on Anne-Marie's lap and beg, "Tell me another story about living in Canada, Anne-Marie. Tell me about snow."

He'd never seen snow, never built a snowman, never made snow angels, poor, deprived darling.

Once, when he caught her drying her hair after a swim, he leaned against her and said sadly, "*Maman* had gold hair like yours, but she went away. Papa says you'll go away, as well, but I wish you wouldn't. I'll miss you."

"I don't have to go yet," she told him, knowing it was small comfort. "We still have lots of time to spend together. And when I do go home, I'll send you pictures of my house and garden, so you'll know where I live."

He looked at her for a long time, his dark eyes wide and solemn, then buried his face against her shoulder. "It won't be the same," he said, his voice muffled and quivering. But he didn't shed a single tear because he already knew that crying wasn't enough to make a person stay. It broke her heart that he'd learned such a hard lesson so early in life.

Later, when she thought he'd forgotten all about their conversation, he asked, "I can read a bit. Will you write letters to me, as well? I like it when I get mail. The mail-man brought me lots of cards on my birthday.''

''I'll send you lots of letters,'' she promised. ''And just so that you get them faster, I'll e-mail them to you on your daddy's computer.''

''No. Papa might be angry. He says I shouldn't keep bothering you.''

''Then I'll send them to Solange instead, and it'll be our little secret.''

It wasn't the only secret she kept from Ethan. The first evening of her new regime, after she'd finished work, she wanted to stretch her cramped muscles before turning in, and decided to explore the gardens. That was how she found the rough-hewn steps leading down the cliff.

At the bottom was a quiet cove, a perfect crescent of white sand with a big flat rock in the middle where she sat for the longest time, watching the moon rise over the sea. On her return, she almost bumped into Philippe as he materialized silently from the shadows on the far side of the pool, and let himself into Solange's villa.

Every night after that, Anne-Marie went down to the beach, aware that under cover of dark, Philippe sneaked down to spend the night with his fiancée. Solange was not sleeping alone, whatever Ethan might like to think, and he'd be furious if he ever found out.

Anne-Marie wasn't all that thrilled, herself. The smallest sound carried clearly on the quiet air and try as she might, she couldn't help hearing the muffled laughter from next door, or the murmured voices, or, worst of all, the smoth-ered moans.

She was, she realized with disgust, jealous. Jealous of her friend's happiness. Jealous that Solange had someone to love, when she had not.

Then, just after ten on the fifth night, with Solange's

place already in darkness, Ethan showed up at Anne-Marie's door. "I saw the light on and thought I'd stop by," he said. "Are you still working?"

He wore a shirt made of some lightweight, oatmeal-colored fabric, matching drawstring pants, and black molded Teva sandals. She, on the other hand, had just stepped out of the shower. She was barefoot, wore a thin cotton robe which barely covered her knees, and her hair was wrapped in a towel turban.

Of course! I always dress like this to work, she was tempted to reply, but decided she was in no position to be saucy. He might be dressed casually, but at least he looked decent which was more than could be said for her. "No," she said mildly. "I'm done for the day."

"Then may I come in? I'd like to talk to you."

Given that he already had one foot inside the door and wasn't about to pay the least mind to any objection she might raise, she moved aside in tacit consent. "About what?"

"First off, my son." The foyer was just large enough for a couple to tango if they felt so inclined, but it shrank to insignificant proportions under the aura of disapproval radiating from his imposing six-foot-plus frame. "He's spending altogether too much time with you."

"I enjoy his company."

"If it's company you're looking for, there's plenty to be had at the main house."

"Then let me rephrase it. I *prefer* his company."

"To my aunt and uncle's?"

"No," she said. "To yours."

His mouth twitched with amusement. "I'm crushed, my dear! But I'll survive—and so will you. Adrian, however, is a different matter. *He* is far too vulnerable to be left to your mercies."

''What are you afraid of?'' she exclaimed incredulously. ''You can't seriously believe I'd do anything to hurt him?''

''Not intentionally, perhaps, but however well-intentioned your motives, in the long run you'll end up doing him more harm than good.''

''For heaven's sake, Ethan, I don't rot his teeth by feeding him sugar, or teach him foul language, or let him wander off into the jungle unsupervised! He's never in the pool unless Solange is with him because I know I'm useless in the event of a water emergency. All I do I *play* with him.''

''I know,'' he said, loping past her to take a turn about the salon, and pausing to admire the shimmering aquamarine fabric laid out on the worktable. ''But he's not a toy, Anne-Marie. And he doesn't understand the games played by women like you.''

There wasn't another man on earth who could match his ability to put her back up and leave her so angry she could almost smell smoke! ''What's that supposed to mean— *women like me?*''

He stopped before the dress form to inspect the beadwork on the bodice of Solange's wedding gown. ''The fly-by-night kind who flits without warning or reason from one obsession to another. Right now, you're enjoying the adulation of one small, impressionable boy, but once the novelty wears off and his neediness becomes a burden, you'll drop him and move on to the next thing to catch your fancy, without any thought for the hurt you'll inflict on him.''

''You must be confusing me with your ex-wife,'' she said acidly. ''I wouldn't dream of treating a child, or any other living creature, for that matter, as shabbily as you seem to think.''

''Leave my ex-wife out of it!''

''Why should I, when we both know she's smack in the middle of it?'' she retorted, prepared to go toe-to-toe with him on this one. ''You're saddling me with her failings and holding me accountable for them.''

''Can you blame me? You're part of that glitzy, artificial world that lured her away from here in the first place.''

''To assume that makes me glitzy and artificial is a bit of a stretch, don't you think?''

''We're reflections of our tastes and inclinations, *Mademoiselle*,'' he said, making his way to where she stood.

''Oh, good grief, are we back to the *mademoiselle* nonsense again?'' She smacked him smartly on the shoulder which probably wasn't the wisest thing she could have done, but it beat rapping him on his thick skull, which was what she really felt like doing. ''Well, listen up, *Monsieur!* Believe it or not as you please, but I'm not in the habit of treating people as disposable commodities. Having known firsthand how it feels to be left with virtually no one, I treasure friendship above all else and I'm sincerely fond of Adrian. I fail to see how anyone could not be. He's adorable.''

''He's fond of you, too. That's my whole point. He misses his mother and is constantly looking for someone to take her place. But you're only a temporary fixture in his life and how your leaving will affect him isn't something you'll have to deal with. I'm the one responsible for his happiness and well-being, which is why I'm taking steps now to protect him from you.''

''Are you forbidding me to associate with him?'' she asked hotly. ''Because if you are, I want your word that you'll explain it to him without making me out to be the villain of the piece. I won't have him think I've abandoned him by choice.''

''There's no need to take quite such drastic steps. He understands you have work to do and that he can't disturb you whenever the mood takes him. All I'm asking is that, instead of fostering this close one-on-one relationship which, ultimately, must come to an end, you instead spend time with him at the main house and become part of our larger family group. Which brings me to my second point. You *do* recall there were two matters I wished to discuss?''

''Sweet heaven, how could I possibly forget? I've been waiting with breathless anticipation for the other shoe to drop!'' She lowered her lashes and sighed with deliberately melodramatic emphasis. ''All right. I'm braced for the worst. Let me have it, and don't spare my feelings.''

''You've been avoiding me.''

''Is it any wonder?''

Purposefully, he stepped closer, and the expression in his eyes made her quake a little inside. If ever there was a man on a mission, he was it! ''Do you think avoiding me is going to change what happened between us the other night, Anne-Marie?''

''No,'' she said, not so transfixed that she wasn't woefully conscious of how absurd he must find her, in her tooshort robe and too-large towel turban which made her head look at least three times bigger than it ought to be. ''But not having to see you helps me to put the whole unfortunate incident into perspective. I didn't come here looking to have an affair.''

''I don't recall suggesting you did.''

''You might as well have! From the way you kissed me—''

He shrugged. ''I'm no saint, Anne-Marie. When a beautiful woman makes it plain she's both willing and available, I'm as susceptible as the next man to what she's offering.''

It was as bad as she'd feared! He'd interpreted the moment all too accurately, right down to her practically throwing herself at him. "You're also more imaginative than most!" she snapped, humiliated. "We kissed—*kissed*, Ethan, and by mutual consent at that, so don't make it out to be more than it was—a colossal, foolish mistake."

"Exactly—as I believe I said, both before and after the fact."

"I ought to have guessed you'd be an *I told you so* kind of man."

"But I have been known to be wrong on occasion." A slow smile crept over his mouth, and try as she might, she couldn't drag her gaze away from it, or quell the rising heat in her blood as he covered the remaining distance between them.

"You have?" she squeaked.

"Indeed yes. You look very appealing in that thing, by the way." He hooked a finger between the buttons on the front of her robe and tugged her even closer. If he'd touched her skin, she swore she'd have burst into flames. "But *this* doesn't do a thing for you."

Before she could guess his next move, he'd unwound the towel from her head and was running his hands through her hair. "There," he said, his voice about as seductive a purr as she'd ever heard. "That's much better. Hair such as yours should never be hidden from sight."

"I don't think you should be doing that," she protested faintly, as he continued massaging her scalp. "I think it could lead to our making another really colossal mistake."

"Or not," he murmured, moving in for the kill. "It depends on your point of view."

She'd wondered often enough over the last few days if memory had played her false; if it had blown the other night out of all proportion and left her vulnerable to huge disappointment, should there ever be another such encounter. As his mouth came down on hers a second time, though, she learned the folly of such thinking. If that first kiss had taken her by surprise, this one took her by storm. More deliberate, less cautious, it caught her up in a deluge of sensory pleasure so intense that the world tilted on its axis.

Nor, for once, was he entirely in command of the universe. His mouth was hot and possessive, his hands hot and urgent as they traced down her back from her neck to her hips. In truth, he was hot and hard all over, a fact made glaringly apparent by the flimsiness of the clothing separating their two bodies.

And she, clinging to him for fear that she'd melt in a puddle at his feet if she let go, wanted to submit to his implicit demands, and never mind that they barely knew each other and didn't much like what they'd so far discovered. Because Solange had been right. All that superficial animosity had been nothing more than camouflage to mask the attraction which had exploded between them with the suddenness and force of spontaneous combustion.

If, rather than meeting him formally amid the grandeur of his estate, she had instead come across him in a street market, the outcome would have been the same. She didn't need to know his name, nor he hers. He didn't have to be rich and powerful, nor she successful and independent. They could have been beggars, and still the *only* reality that would have mattered was the primal knowledge that, somehow, out of all the other men and women in the world, they had recognized each other.

This is insane! You're both crazy!

The admonishment fought to surface in her befuddled mind, and was swamped. What chance had reason against such elemental force?

None at all! She was ready to yield to him completely, there on the cool marble floor of the foyer, and hang the consequences. But even as a whimper of surrender rose in her throat, another, fraught with equal passion, floated faintly through the night and turned her rigid with trepidation.

"Oh!" she moaned, loud enough to drown out the other sound, and then, just to be on the safe side, "Oh, oh, oh!"

If she'd hoped to distract him, she succeeded, but hardly in the way she'd hoped. He lifted his head, stared at her as if she'd lost her mind, and said coldly, "You sound pained. Is it because of something you ate?"

"No," she said, embarrassed.

"Then it must be me. I had no idea you found my attentions so unappealing."

The next moment, she was alone, feeling so let down and frustrated that she could barely stand.

CHAPTER SIX

AN INVITATION to afternoon tea with Josephine arrived at Anne-Marie's door the following day, and turned out to be such a mutually pleasant event that it became a daily ritual after that. Sometimes Solange joined the party, and Adrian was always there, hopping with impatience for his new best friend to put in an appearance.

The refreshments, served in the shade of a verandah overlooking the hummingbird garden, consisted of an array of delicacies wheeled out on a trolley, to where Josephine presided at a low table set with snowy linen and a magnificent sterling tea set.

"Ethan's mother started the tradition," she explained, one day when Solange had gone to visit friends with Philippe, and Adrian, bored with too much grown-up talk, had wandered off into the garden to play with his kitten. "She was born in London, you see, and although her father was a doctor on Saint Vincent, here in the Caribbean, she grew up in England and held its customs very dear to her heart."

Anne-Marie helped herself to a buttery scone heaped with imported preserves and clotted cream. "How did she happen to meet Ethan's father?"

"She came out here on holiday when she turned nineteen and met him at the races in Barbados—horse races, that is. They're very big in this part of the world. You must get Ethan to show you his stables, someday when you're not both tied up with work."

"I'd like that." Not that there was any chance she'd

ever get it! She'd seen neither hide nor hair of him since the night he'd stopped by. At first seeming as helplessly attracted to her as she was to him, he'd initiated a kiss that fairly singed the already steamy night.

But her attempt to cover up what was going on in Solange's quarters had soon put paid to that, and the worst of it was, Anne-Marie had been able to offer no reasonable explanation for her sudden, inexplicable behavior. If only he was more approachable, less inflexible, she might have tried, but that was like wishing for snow on Bellefleur—a notion too fanciful to be entertained.

Josephine handed her a wide-lipped cup balanced on its saucer as gracefully as a lotus blossom floating on water, the china so translucent, a person could almost read print through it. "Earl Grey today, my dear. I hope it's to your taste. Help yourself to lemon, if you prefer."

"Thank you." She sipped the hot, fragrant liquid, and found it delightfully refreshing despite the tropical heat visibly shimmering above the flower beds beyond the verandah. "And they fell in love?"

Josephine blinked. "Who? Oh, André and Patricia, you mean? She was a Hythe-Griffiths, you know, of Griffiths pharmaceutical fame. Very well to do, very aristocratic. And André—well, the Beaumonts are the *crème de la crème* in these parts. Ethan's great-grandfather bought this island in 1921. It had been a French territory before that and was in very sad shape. A few fields of cotton, some peas and corn, wild cattle and sheep—nothing you'd want to live with nowadays, I can assure you. But he rescued it from neglect and turned it into a viable community. Have another scone, child. They'll only go to waste if you don't eat them."

"And Patricia?" Anne-Marie prodded, her curiosity about Ethan's background itching to be satisfied.

"I'm getting to that part. My father was a profligate. When he took over, he drank away the family fortune and let the island fall back into decay, so it was a blessing all around when his horse threw him and broke his neck, because that left André, my younger brother and Ethan's father, in control."

"I see." Anne-Marie hid a smile. Clearly, her hostess was not one to waste sympathy on those she deemed to be undeserving!

"André slaved to restore Bellefleur," Josephine continued. "All those citrus groves and coconut palms you passed, the day you arrived here, are part of his legacy, as are the cotton plantations. He built the roads, an airstrip, a school. And he started a horse breeding program which is what took him to Barbados."

"Where he met Patricia."

"Exactly. It was love at first sight for both of them. She was a beauty, a true English rose, and André...." Josephine sighed, her dark eyes misty with fond memory. "Oh, he was handsome! All the eligible women on Bellefleur wept a little when he brought home a bride. Ethan looks very much like him, but he has his mother's eyes."

"You say André *was* handsome. I take it that means...?"

"Restoring this island to prosperity eventually killed him. He worked himself to death." She blinked, and stroked the wedding ring on her left hand. "And he did it on purpose, because he didn't care to go on living."

"And Patricia?"

"Died in childbirth, a year after she came to Bellefleur as a bride. A terrible tragedy. It never should have happened. But we had no hospital here at the time that she went into labor, and a wicked storm had blown in from the Atlantic, which made getting off the island impossible.'' She sighed. ''It was only after Ethan was born that André built the medical facility, and named it after her. Too little, too late, as the saying goes.''

''Poor man. He must have been heartbroken.''

''More than that, it broke his spirit. He blamed himself for his wife's death, and became frighteningly withdrawn for months afterward. But he had a baby to look out for, a son who needed a mother, and I didn't live here then because Louis's work kept us in Europe. So, two years later, André remarried. Celine was a good woman, a devoted wife. She gave him another son, Philippe.''

''How did Ethan feel about that?''

''Oh, he was thrilled! He was five at the time, and had no memory of Patricia, remember. Celine was the only mother he'd ever known, so there was none of the resentment you might have expected from an older child who'd seen another woman come in and take his birth mother's place. He was very protective of his baby brother.''

''And yet, from your tone and expression, it seems there was no happy ending for this new family.''

Josephine sighed again. ''I'm afraid not. Celine loved André deeply, and he loved her, too, after a fashion, but not the way he'd loved Patricia. Celine knew it, and she was proud. She grew tired of competing with a ghost and always being second best, so she left when Philippe was eight. André wouldn't let her take the boy, and because she was Roman Catholic, divorce was out of the question, so she joined a French convent as a lay person, and took the veil after she became a widow, seven years after that. Ethan was twenty when his father died and left him to take charge not just of the island, but of Philippe, too, who was a very unruly teenager.''

A faint sound overlaying the soft whir of the ceiling fan

in the room behind had both women looking over their shoulders to find Ethan standing in the open doorway, blatantly eavesdropping. "I can't imagine our guest cares one iota about our family saga, Josephine," he said stiffly, his glance skating over Anne-Marie with stunning disregard.

"On the contrary," she said. "I'm enjoying hearing about the Beaumonts and their doings."

"Why?" He flung the question at her baldly, resentfully.

In the hope that it might persuade you I'm not quite as reptilian as you seem to find me, she nearly told him, shivering in the cool blast of his indifference. "Family histories always fascinate me, I suppose because I have so little of my own."

"I didn't know you were back already." Josephine extended her hand in welcome. "Have a cup of tea with us, *mon cher,* and tell us about your trip."

So he'd been away and hadn't necessarily been avoiding her, after all! An untoward flush of pleasure rippled over Anne-Marie, but it barely had time to register before he squashed it.

"I was able to take care of the problem in a matter of hours," he said, accepting the cup his aunt offered and looking out at the sweep of jungle and ocean beyond the garden.

"You were up very early this morning. It was still dark when I heard the car leave."

"Did I disturb you? I'm sorry."

"I never sleep well when I know you're en route to the oil platform. That whole operation makes me very uneasy."

The smile he turned on his aunt, warm and full of teasing affection, filled Anne-Marie with envy. "You don't like having an oil baron in the family?"

"I don't see the necessity for it. We're Caribbean land-owners, not Arabian sheikhs."

But he could have passed for one, Anne-Marie thought, sneaking a look at him as he stood surveying his tiny kingdom. *A blue-eyed western sheikh, as proud and powerful as his desert counterpart.*

"Running Bellefleur costs money, *Tante* Josephine. We have an obligation to the future generations of this island."

"Your father relied on its natural resources."

"They're no longer enough. And I enjoy the change of pace."

"Do you?" she replied tartly, clearly put out at having her opinion dismissed. "Well, Anne-Marie could use a change of pace, too. She's working much too hard. I told her you'd show her the stables."

Once again, his cool gaze drifted over Anne-Marie. "I doubt she's really interested."

Anger rushed in to take the place of that wayward flash of optimism. "Why don't you try asking me, instead of behaving as if I'm a piece of furniture incapable of speaking for myself?"

He raised one arrogant eyebrow. "Do you ride?"

"Not as well as you, probably," she said. "But I'm as capable as the next person of appreciating a fine animal."

"You know what to look for in a horse, do you?"

"Besides two legs more than you possess, and a head more handsome?"

He grimaced, annoyed, but Josephine let out a squawk of laughter. "Child, you are a breath of fresh air, and just what this man needs to remind him there's more to life than work!" she crowed, tossing down her embroidered napkin. "Help me up, Ethan. It's time for my pre-dinner siesta."

"I expect you have to go, too," he said hopefully to Anne-Marie, once his aunt had left.

"I suppose I do." Bereft, she brushed a few crumbs from her skirt, and drifted toward the steps leading to the garden.

"You can find your way?"

"Certainly. I've become quite familiar with the layout of the grounds."

"And the wedding gown? Is it finished yet?"

"Not quite. I ran short of seed pearls and am waiting for more to be sent from Vancouver."

"I hope you didn't rely on them arriving by ordinary parcel post."

"No. I always use a courier."

"That's good. Because mail delivery to the island is unreliable, to say the least."

Such inconsequential conversation seemed out of character for a man who, a moment before, had been insultingly anxious to see the back of her. "What's the purpose of these delaying tactics, Ethan?" she inquired boldly. "Is there something else you'd like to say to me that has a relevant purpose beyond wasting both your time and mine?"

"Not at all," he said, staring out at the landscape.

"If you're worried that I've ignored your edict that I stay away from Adrian, don't be."

"I'm not," he said, apparently engrossed by the hummingbirds fighting each other to feed at the flower beds. "It never occurs to me that my requests will go ignored. That being the case, and since you're at a temporary standstill with the wedding project, I'll expect you at the stables at nine tomorrow."

"Then brace yourself for an upset, because this is one time your expectations aren't going to be met. I'm still busy with the bridesmaids' dresses, and can't afford to waste the morning.''

It was a lie. Apart from final finishing, the dresses were done and, for once, she had the luxury of time on her hands—a rare occurrence when she was at home, with the phone constantly ringing and new designs being commissioned daily. But his implicit censure of everything she said or did cast a long shadow and took the shine off the bright afternoon.

Why expose herself to more of the same, tomorrow? She still had several weeks left on the island and she wanted to enjoy them. Why let him strip her of the pleasure?

''That's a pity. Some other day, perhaps?''

She shrugged. ''Perhaps,'' she said, matching his nonchalance, and without bothering to spare him another word or glance, set off across the lawn.

The dazzling, sun-splashed days and scented, star-spangled nights fell into a pattern of lazy indulgences. At least three times daily, she swam in the guest pool. She took tea with Josephine. She drew pictures for Adrian, and played croquet with Louis. She and Solange lazed in recliners on the shaded walkway connecting their suites, and sipped tall, cool drinks while they reminisced about old times. Before she went to bed, she walked down to the beach and sat on her favorite rock to watch the moon rise, and soak in the tranquility and beauty of the sleeping island.

Apart from showing up each night for dinner, Ethan kept his distance, but that didn't lessen her infatuation with him. The meal tended to be long and leisurely, often lasting two or more hours but, no matter how delicious the food or entertaining the conversation, they couldn't compete with him.

Sometimes, she feared the memory of him sitting at the

head of the table in that spectacularly elegant dining room, his immaculate white dinner jacket in gleaming contrast to the burnished bronze of his skin, his rare smile bringing life and youth to his often somber face, would stay with her the rest of her life and make it impossible for any other man to take his place.

Nor was he as oblivious to her as he tried to make out. Occasionally—*very* occasionally!—they'd share a moment's amusement at something Josephine said, but most of the time he treated Anne-Marie with distant courtesy.

Yet for all that he tried to hide it, she was sublimely conscious of his gaze resting on her when he thought she wasn't looking. Once, she caught him at it, and he immediately lowered his eyes and scowled at the broiled pheasant in front of him, as if the poor thing had risen up from the dead and laid an egg on his plate!

All that being so, she was surprised to receive a phone call from him at the beginning of her fourth week on the island. "A replacement part for some machinery which I ordered from the mainland arrived this morning, and I'm headed out to the airport to pick it up," he told her. "You want to come with me? There's a package waiting there for you, as well."

"Yes," she said, the chance to be alone with him, for however short a time, more than she could resist.

"Meet me in the front courtyard in half an hour, then," he said. "And wear a hat. The heat's enough to kill you today, and I'd hate for you to get sunstroke."

No "please," or "will you," but his concern for her well-being took the sting out of his command. Hanging up the phone, she hurried to exchange the knee-length sarong she always wore around the guest quarters for a gauzy cotton dress in pale apple green sprigged with tiny pink rosebuds, and a wide-brimmed straw hat.

''You look delicious as a sherbet sundae,'' he surprised her by saying, when he saw her. ''All cool and shady, except for your skin. You've picked up quite a tan.''

She'd have told him he looked entirely fabulous himself, if his compliment hadn't left her tongue-tied. What a mass of contradictions he was; charming one minute, and chillingly aloof the next. How was a woman supposed to know where she stood with him?

He walked her out to the forecourt and handed her into a white Rolls Royce Corniche. Fairly tingling from his touch, she said, ''Is Adrian coming with us?''

''No. He's in school.''

''I didn't know he attended school. I suppose he has a private tutor?''

''You suppose wrong. He goes to the local school, but only in the morning. He's still in kindergarten. Have you had a chance to explore the town, at all?''

''No.''

He put on a pair of sunglasses and nosed the stunningly elegant convertible down the steep driveway. The big iron gates swung smoothly open as the car approached, then glided closed once it had passed through. ''I'll show you the sights, after we've collected our stuff. I assume the package waiting for you is the beading you need to finish Solange's dress?''

''I hope so. The wedding's fast approaching.''

''We'll fly to Florida and shop in Miami, if necessary. One way or another, you'll have your supplies.''

''I hope it won't come to that, but it's very nice of you to be so accommodating.''

''Not really,'' he replied, dashing any hope she had that winning a few Brownie points with her was his prime objective. ''It's a Beaumont wedding. It has to be perfect.''

''Of course! Silly me, to have thought for one second

that it might be because you were willing to go out of your way on my behalf.''

His expression inscrutable behind the reflective lens of his glasses, he said, ''The two go hand in hand, surely? The guest list runs close to three hundred and all those people will see your work and no doubt admire it enough that some will want you to design for them. This could be a real boost for your career.''

''I don't need a boost, thank you very much,'' she said. ''I already have more than enough clients.''

''Aren't you interested in seeing your company grow?''

They were passing through the town by then and the open car afforded her an unobstructed view of the quaint conical roofs on the houses, and the pretty flowering vines climbing over fences and doorways. Down near the quay, a street market hummed with shoppers clustered around stalls loaded with fresh fish, fruit, vegetables, and other food.

The kaleidoscope of color, bright orange, red and yellow against a backdrop of azure sky and turquoise water, added to the scent of blossoms mingling with fresh baked bread and the sharp tang of the ocean, presented a feast to the senses like nothing she'd experienced before. And yet, despite the bustle of activity, the pace of life was so much less frenetic than what she was used to in Vancouver.

Here, people really did take time to smell the flowers. Here, there was always tomorrow on which to take care of the things that didn't get done today.

''Well, Anne-Marie? *Don't* you want to increase your business assets?''

''No,'' she said, surprising herself almost as much as she no doubt surprised him. ''I love my work, but it doesn't consume me, nor does it fill all the corners of my life. It never will.''

"How so?"

Again, she surprised herself. "Because, at the end of my life when I look back at what I've achieved, costume design won't be what counts."

"And what will?"

"A real home."

"You don't have one?" He sounded skeptical.

"I have a very smart town house, if that's what you mean. It's extremely comfortable, very well located, quite charming, and it suits me well enough for now. But I want to be remembered for something more meaningful than a pile of lumber and a few dramatic designs which will be forgotten even sooner than I will. I want to leave behind a legacy of love."

"And just how do you propose to do that?"

"With a family," she said, her heart swelling with a need which went back twenty years, to the day she'd learned she was an orphan. "With a husband and children."

He turned onto the road leading to the airport. "Successful career woman giving it all up for the dubious joy of changing diapers and scrubbing floors? Somehow, I don't see you fitting into such a picture—unless, of course, you plan to marry for money."

She could have slapped him. He certainly deserved it. "Did I forget to mention that I don't need to go searching for a rich husband? That I have enough in the way of assets that I can afford to marry a poor man and the only criteria is that he love me for myself, and not for what I own?"

"Is that ever enough to keep a woman happy?"

Annoyed, she threw the question back at him. "Is it enough for men?"

"Yes," he said. "Often to their lasting regret. Because

most men are very straightforward about their objectives, whereas women too often have an ulterior motive.''

An invisible cloud seemed to pass over the bright day. ''Are we talking about your ex-wife again?''

''She fits the type, certainly.''

She longed to ask him what the woman had done to disillusion him so thoroughly, but sensed he'd rebuff her. Instead, she said, ''Do you think Solange has an ulterior motive in marrying your brother?''

''Solange is different.''

''We're *all* different, Ethan, that's my whole point, and you're too smart a person to make such dangerously sweeping statements and really believe them. We have minds of our own, we choose how to live our lives, and sometimes we make mistakes. But most of us learn from them and go on to make wiser choices in the future.''

He brought the Corniche to a stop outside the small terminal. The sun scorched blinding white on the tarmac. The heat hung in the air, dense and breathless. He swung open his door and climbed out. ''And some of us don't,'' he said flatly. ''Some *mistakes* as you choose to call them, are unforgivable. Are you coming in, or do you want to wait here?''

''I'll come in,'' she said, wilting under his unflagging bitterness. How he must have loved his wife, that she'd been able to wound him so deeply!

CHAPTER SEVEN

SHE played her part well, that much he had to give her. Hardly ever a false step and even when she stumbled, a man had to have his wits about him to notice. And therein lay the problem because, when he was around her, his wits took second place to other, more primitive instincts.

"We'll have lunch at the Plantation Club," he said, when the business at the airport was done. "It overlooks the yacht basin and if there's a breeze to be found anywhere, it'll be there."

"Sounds lovely," she said demurely, dipping her head so that her face was hidden under the brim of her hat, and if he hadn't known better, he might have been fooled into thinking she was shy.

The club was crowded, as usual, but he had a permanent reservation and they were led to his table immediately. Fully aware of the interest aroused by his appearing with a stranger who swept into the place with her pale green skirt swirling just above her ankles like the sudden onset of a cool Canadian spring, he nodded to the familiar faces already at lunch and, wanting to observe her reaction to the stir she'd created, sat her in the corner and took the chair next to her, so that they both looked out at the room.

"Iced tea," she replied, when he asked her what she'd like to drink.

"Try the planter's punch instead," he suggested. "You'll find it very refreshing." And before she could voice a protest, ordered one for each of them.

She took off her hat and dropped it carelessly next to

her straw bag on the floor. "Are you going to choose my food, as well?" she wanted to know, the impudence he found so attractive sparkling in her eyes.

"As a matter of fact, yes." She'd wound her hair up on top of her head, but a strand had fallen loose and spilled down the nape of her neck like a skein of pale silk ribbon on a honey-gold background. Suppressing the urge to tuck it back into place, he nodded at the waiter who'd served both his father and grandfather before him. "We'll have the conch salad, Hamilton."

The man took off to the bar, and returned a short time later with the drinks. After he left a second time, she ran a finger lightly down her throat and turned her head to catch the drift of breeze created by the overhead fans. "You were right," she said. "It is much cooler here."

"I'm glad you approve."

A smile tugged at her mouth. "Aren't you going to tell me you're always right?"

"I'm only right ninety-nine point nine percent of the time."

The smile gave way to a teasing laugh, a bewitching musical fall of amusement that captivated him. "You mean, you once thought you'd made a mistake, but you were wrong?" Then, touching her fingers to her mouth, said contritely, "Oh, I'm sorry! That wasn't a very nice thing to say, and I really didn't mean it!"

"Why do I have trouble believing that?"

"I think because you and I become very good at not saying what we really mean, Ethan. Very good at leaping to all the wrong conclusions about each other." She clinked the rim of her glass against his. "How about a toast to not doing that anymore?"

The memory of their last kiss surfaced in his mind, right down to the artificial moans of ecstasy she'd let out. Too bad she'd had her eyes wide open at the time, and looked more like a terrified mare about to be mated with a raging stallion, than a woman wildly overcome with passion! "Is that possible?"

"We could always try, couldn't we?"

"For what purpose?"

"Well, you said yourself that we can't avoid each other. Why make things any more awkward than they have to be?" She sipped her punch. "This is delicious, by the way. If the conch salad's half as good, I'm going to have to swallow my pride and let you do all the ordering in future."

"For the remainder of your time here, at least," he said, his attention caught by the silhouette of the man poised on the threshold leading from the outside deck. Although backlit by the early afternoon sun, there was no mistaking his identity.

So, Roberto Santos was back on Bellefleur!

Ethan fixed him in a stare, and silently dared him to acknowledge it. Santos stood a moment, scanning the tables, then, sensing he was being observed, his glance swiveled and collided with Ethan's.

His mouth twitched, the full, almost feminine lips tightening a fraction. He tilted his head, aiming for arrogance, but the attempt wilted under his enemy's unblinking regard. Aware that just about everyone else present was interested in how he was going to handle the situation, he squared his shoulders and wove a jaunty path among the tables until he reached Ethan's.

"It has been a long time," he said, the heavily-accented English some people found so irresistible more pronounced than ever. "How are you, *amigo?*"

"Like most people on the island, better off not having to share it with you. What brings you back here, Santos?"

"What always brings me back? The beautiful ladies, of course," he drawled insolently, bending an oily smirk on Anne-Marie who lowered her too-long, too-dark lashes, and smiled back prettily. "Are you going to introduce me to your lovely companion?"

"No. That's a privilege I reserve for friends and you hardly qualify. You're not looking your usual buff self, Santos. Prison didn't agree with you?"

An ugly flush darkened the man's face. "I see that trying to smooth over our differences was a mistake. You are clearly a man who prefers to hold on to a grudge." He clicked his heels and gave a stiff little bow. "Good day, *Señorita!* Perhaps we'll meet another time, under happier circumstances."

"Not if I have anything to say about it," Ethan assured him.

Looking thunderstruck, Anne-Marie fortified herself with another sip of punch before jumping into the silence left behind as Santos beat a retreat. "Did you have to be quite so cruel? The man was just trying to be sociable."

"Did you not hear me refer to his having been incarcerated?"

"Oh, yes," she said, with heavy sarcasm. "I doubt anyone in the room missed it!"

"Then what makes you think I owe him any sort of courtesy?"

"Maybe the fact that he's served his time and shouldn't have his past held against him any longer?"

"You know nothing about his past. If you did, you might not feel so charitably inclined toward him."

"Perhaps not. But all I know right now is that you were intolerably rude, and went out of your way to humiliate him in front of a roomful of people who obviously know him."

Ethan drew in a long breath, and debated the wisdom of telling her more, because she was right in one respect. The past was over. But if, by keeping his silence, he allowed Santos to come across as the victim rather than the perpetrator, could he live with that?

"He was convicted of impaired driving on a neighboring island," he said brusquely, settling for the short version of the story.

"Oh." She looked down, her expression somber. "Well, I agree, that's hardly to his credit."

"No, it isn't," he said. "Especially not when he had a child in the car at the time of his arrest."

Her gaze, wide with distress, flew back to his face. "Was the child hurt?"

"No. Neither the child nor the mother was injured."

She drew in a shocked breath. "His wife was there, and did nothing to stop him from getting behind the wheel of a car and risking their child's life?"

"It wasn't his wife, nor was it his child. They were mine."

"Oh, Ethan!" Impulsively, she covered his hand. "I'm sorry!"

"Why? You had nothing to do with it."

"But I misjudged you. And so soon after we'd made a pact not to leap to conclusions about each other."

"Actually, we never did reach agreement on that, but it doesn't matter. Santos doesn't matter, either, not any more, and he's not worth spoiling our lunch over. Here comes our salad. Would you care for another rum punch?"

"Good grief, no! I've hardly touched this one, and already it's going to my head. I'd like some water, though."

He ordered a bottle of Perrier, and turned the conversation in another direction. "The package you picked up were the beads you need to finish Solange's wedding gown?''

''Yes,'' she said, her attention caught by something or someone beyond his view. Well, what had he expected? That she'd hang on his every word as if she really cared about anything he had to say? She was every bit as shallow as he'd first supposed, and any inclination he might have had to change his mind on that had died the other night. ''They had to be ordered specially, which is what took so long for them to arrive, but now that they're here, I'll have the dress done in no time.''

''Then perhaps once it's finished, you'll change your mind and take me up on my invitation to visit the stables.''

''Perhaps I will,'' she said vaguely, her glance again sliding past him.

''What's so intriguing, Anne-Marie? Don't tell me Santos is still hanging around, ogling you from afar?''

''No,'' she said. ''But a woman just came in the door and from the way she keeps looking over here, I think she must recognize you. In fact, I'm certain she does because she's headed right this way.''

He glanced up in time to see Desirée LaSalle approaching. Following so soon after Santos's unwelcome visit, it was something he could have done without.

''It *is* you, Ethan!'' she warbled. ''I was sure I must be mistaken.''

''Have I changed that much since the last time you saw me?'' he said lightly, standing up and kissing the proffered, perfumed cheek.

She stepped back and pursed her lips in a pretty pout. ''Well, it has been weeks, *Chéri*. And I hardly expected…''

That he'd be with another woman? She might as well have come out and said what she was so clearly thinking. Her hazel-eyed glance, as it slid dismissively over Anne-Marie, spoke volumes of protest.

Knowing he couldn't very well refuse an introduction this time, he said, "I'd like you to meet Solange's maid of honor, Anne-Marie Barclay. This is Desirée LaSalle, Anne-Marie."

"Oh, she's the seamstress! I've already heard about her from Angelique. Well, aren't you a sweetie, treating her to lunch at a place like this, Ethan." Desirée slid a familiar arm through his, her pout melting in the sudden warmth of the smile she turned on Anne-Marie. "Is the sewing going well, dear?"

"Oh, yes, ever so!" Anne-Marie cooed, too sweetly for his peace of mind. "Thank you so much for asking! And I'm ever so grateful to *Monsieur* Beaumont for letting me take a few hours off and showing me the sights. It's a real honor."

"I'm glad you realize what a very lucky woman you are. Ethan doesn't usually bother to squire the hired help around the island."

"Are you here alone, Desirée?" he asked, not liking the direction the conversation had taken, or the crackling tension that went with it.

"Actually not." She bathed him in another smile. "I'm with friends."

"Well, don't let us keep you from them."

"They won't mind. They won't even miss me, if you're thinking of asking me to join you."

"Some other time, perhaps. We're about ready to leave," he said, hurriedly detaching himself from her grasp. "If you're finished toying with that salad, Anne-Marie…?"

"Quite," she said, the frost in her voice rivaling the ice cubes clinking in her water glass. "I find I don't have as much of an appetite as I first thought. In fact, I believe I have a touch of indigestion.''

"Too much sun, perhaps," Desirée suggested.

"Too much hot air, certainly," she replied, plunking her hat on her head and disappearing behind the brim.

"Feel up to a stroll to help settle your stomach?" he asked snidely, once they were outside.

"Not if you're in a hurry to get back."

"I wouldn't have offered, if I was. We'll go as far as the market, and give you a taste of local life."

"Whatever." She shrugged indifferently.

"Do you like sailing?"

"No. Why do you ask?"

"Because I own the white yacht moored at the end of the second dock over there, and I'd offer to take you for an evening cruise, but if you're not interested...."

"Perhaps you've forgotten already how my parents died," she said icily. "But if it's company you're looking for, I'm sure Ms. LaSalle would be more than happy to join you."

"I apologize," he said, truly contrite. "That was insensitive, even for me."

"Fine," she replied, and sank into stony silence.

They walked in silence for another hundred yards or so, then turned down a narrow lane enclosed on both sides by high walls beyond which ornamental palms clacked and swayed in the breeze.

Still cursing himself for being so thoughtless, he tried again to engage her in conversation. "Some of the oldest residences on the island lie along here," he said. "Fine houses set in beautiful gardens. You'll see one for yourself in a few days. The Tourneaus are throwing a pre-wedding party on the Thursday before the wedding. You've already met their daughter, Angelique. She's the other brides-maid.''

Another silence ensued. Finally, she said, ''You're sleeping with her, aren't you?''

''Who, Angelique Tourneau? Good God, no! Why would you even ask such a question?''

''Not her,'' she snapped. ''She's much too charming and well-bred! I'm talking about the other one. That LaSalle creature.''

''Desirée's harmless, Anne-Marie.''

''She's a viper in panty hose!''

''Well, not that it's any of your business,'' he said, hardly able to keep his face straight, ''but no, I am not sleeping with her. Nor do I intend to.''

''Why not?''

''Because she's not my type, and she wants more than I'm prepared to give. Now I have a question for you. Why do you care?''

She didn't lie very well. ''I don't,'' she said, turning pink.

''Is that why I had to get you out of the club before you ripped her throat out?''

''I didn't like her condescending attitude,'' she said primly.

''I didn't like the unflattering innuendo in your remarks, a moment ago, either. What do you mean, Angelique's *too charming and well-bred to sleep with me?*''

Her blush deepened to the color of the fuchsia bougain-villea hanging over the wall behind her. ''I didn't mean it quite how it came out.''

''So we're back to that again, are we? Saying one thing, and meaning another?''

''It's your fault!'' she shot back, flustered. ''You make me do and say things I don't mean, all the time.''

"I guess that explains your phony, melodramatic response to my kiss, the other night."

Her mouth dropped open. "I liked being kissed by you!" she exclaimed, on an indignant puff of breath.

"Oh, please, Anne-Marie! Save it for someone too inexperienced to know the difference between play-acting, and the real thing."

Her lashes swooped down to hide whatever expression her eyes might betray and, this time, the color stained her throat and neck as well as her face, leaving him wondering how far down it went before it stopped. "How did you know?"

It was the last thing he'd expected her to say. Denials, yes; injured innocence, certainly. But outright admission of guilt? Never! In his experience, few women were capable of that kind of honest introspection.

"That you weren't exactly swept away by the moment?" He shrugged. "Oh, I don't know. The unconvincing moans, perhaps. Or the way you latched onto me and tried to drag me farther inside all the time that your eyes were wide open and filled with something other than overwhelming desire. Shall I go on, or have I made my point?"

She pressed her lips together, reminding him all too vividly of how soft and silky they'd felt under his, and ventured an uncertain glance at him from beneath those absurdly long lashes.

"I'm sorry. I was distracted by...night noises."

Her embarrassment, rather than her words, were what clued him in to what she really meant. "Are you perhaps referring to the goings-on next door?"

She paled a little and nibbled the corner of her mouth. "You mean, you *know?*"

"I'm neither blind nor stupid, Anne-Marie," he said,

wearily, resuming their walk. "I'm fully aware my brother spends most nights with his bride-to-be."

"You are? And you're not doing anything to put a stop to it?"

"They're consenting adults. As long as they're discreet, I'm not going to make a fuss."

"But I thought that was the reason you insisted Solange not stay in the main house. I thought—"

"You thought I was a controlling bully whose chief pleasure in life was wielding his clout to make those around him as miserable as possible."

"Well, you *do* like to have your own way!"

"Where my son is concerned, yes, I do. I will not have him exposed to behavior which will only confuse him. He had enough of that with his mother's carryings-on."

He hadn't realized he'd set such a brisk pace that she was almost running to keep up with him until she caught his arm and said, "Slow down, Ethan, please, and let me catch my breath enough to apologize. I've misjudged you on a number of points and I'm really sorry."

"Are you?"

"Yes. I hate that other things and other people keep coming between us."

"Given that your stay here is temporary, it hardly matters."

"It matters," she said firmly. "Everything matters in life, Ethan. Every ant you step on accidentally, every petal that falls, everything and everyone—especially us."

"Us? How do you figure that?"

"Well, Solange is like a sister to me, so after the wedding, you and I will be...sort of related."

"Related?"

She blushed again, a lovely, delectable shade of rose.

"Stop looking at me like that!" she mumbled. "If *related* is too strong a word for you, how about *friends,* instead?"

She was the kind of woman who eroded a man's defenses. Warm, forgiving, generous, and a damn sight too alluring. If he'd met her seven years ago…!

But that kind of useless thinking did nothing but provoke the urge to kiss her again, and *that* annoyed him enough to say brusquely, "I'm not the kind of man who makes friends casually or easily, Anne-Marie."

"Well, at least we're on speaking terms again. Isn't that progress of a sort?"

"It's a beginning," he allowed.

"And that's enough," she said, lifting her face and bathing him in a smile which threatened to topple what was left of his reserve. "At least for now. Tell me more about the island, Ethan. How does it feel to know you hold the welfare of its residents in the palm of your hand?"

They'd left the old residential section behind by then, and reached the center of town where the market clustered around the fishing harbor. "No different from any other job where a man's responsible for his employees," he said, then stopped to greet the young mother passing by with a baby balanced on her hip. "*Bonjour,* Madeleine! That's a fine-looking boy you've got there. How's your husband?"

"Getting stronger every day, thanks to you, *Monsieur,*" she replied. "The operation saved his life, and we can never repay you for your generosity."

"You already have, Madeleine, by being there when Jean needed you," he told her. "Give him my best, and take care of each other."

"No different from any other job?" Anne-Marie said, watching as Madeleine went on her way. "I rather doubt that."

"I might own the land, but I don't own its people, nor could I run it efficiently without their cooperation."

"But they revere you as if you're a god, and I'm beginning to understand why."

"I'm as mortal as the next man, Anne-Marie. I've made my share of mistakes, and there's not a soul here who doesn't know it."

"Do you ever get claustrophobic, living on such a relatively small patch of land, with everyone knowing your business?"

"I don't," he said, the question giving rise to far more unpleasant memories than she could begin to imagine, "but there are some who do. You might find, if you stay here long enough, that you're one of those people."

"Oh, I don't think so!" She flung out her arms and spun around, sending the skirt of her dress dancing around her slim ankles. "I love the open vistas of sea and sky. There's a feeling of freedom here that I've never experienced anywhere else."

"There's also a lack of sophisticated culture. No opera or theater, or ballet. No glitzy hotels or resorts."

"That's what the rest of the world's for, Ethan, and in this day and age, it's only a short hop away. After all, aren't you the one who said, just this morning, that if my sewing supplies didn't arrive in time, we'd go shopping in Miami? But this…!" She climbed on the low stone wall separating the market from the park behind the beach and, taking off her hat, sent it skimming through the air like a saucer. "This is paradise!"

A boy of about eight, dark-skinned, dark-eyed, dark-haired, left the soccer game he was involved in, picked up her hat from its landing spot on the grass, and ran over to present it to her. *"Pour vous, Mademoiselle."*

"Thank you, angel," she said, jumping down from the

wall and bending so that she was at eye level with him. *"Merci beaucoup!"*

He held her gaze a moment, broke into a worshipful smile, then ran back to join his friends.

"Isn't he beautiful?" she murmured, straightening.

"They all are, at that age," Ethan said, giving in to the stab of regret assailing him at the way she'd addressed the child.

Had any woman ever spoken to Adrian with such a wealth of tenderness in her voice? He thought not. Though loving enough, Josephine wasn't given to extravagant demonstrations of affection, and Lisa.... Lisa had saved her endearments for men outside her marital sphere.

"You sound so sad," Ann-Marie murmured. "Why is that?"

"Because they learn too soon about betrayal, the world stops being a shining, perfect place for them, their innocence is lost, and they never get it back again."

"Not always, Ethan," she said, catching his hand and folding her fingers around his. "There are happy endings, sometimes, and I should think that on this protected, beautiful island, the chances are better than just about anywhere else. There's a sense of family, of belonging here, that you don't find in big cities. It's a wonderful place for a child—safe, free from crime and poverty."

"And still it's not enough for some people."

"It wasn't enough for your ex-wife," she said. "But that was a failing in her, not you."

"Try telling that to Adrian, the next time he wants to know why he doesn't have a mother to come to school concerts, or tuck him in at night, the same as all his friends do. Try answering some of the other questions he asks, as well, while you're at it."

"Well, I don't pretend to be an expert on children," she

said thoughtfully, ''but it seems to me that all you can do is answer as honestly as possible.''

''You think it's that easy, do you?'' He laughed bitterly. ''Then tell me, how should I have answered when my son asked me why his mommy was kissing a man behind the pool cabana and why she wasn't wearing her bikini top at the time?''

''She did *that*?'' Anne-Marie exclaimed, on a shocked intake of breath. ''Oh, Ethan, I'm so sorry! Was she with Señor Santos? Is that why you hate him so much?''

''No. He was just one of several, and when he wound up behind bars, she moved on to a member of my house staff—a blond Adonis responsible for maintaining the swimming pools. They left the island together, just five minutes ahead of my boot, but not before she'd flaunted the affair in front of Adrian.'' He paused long enough to swallow the bitter anger souring his tongue. ''I made up some excuse at the time, but if you think I should now spell it out to him candidly, in all its sordid detail—''

''No, of course I don't! He's too young to understand, and even if he weren't, that's more information than he ever needs to know.''

''Right now, perhaps. But in time he needs to understand, if only to protect himself against repeating my mistake when he's old enough to choose a wife.''

''Why do you assume you're the one who made a mistake?''

''Because I knew the risks, but I married her anyway.''

''When two people are deeply in love, risks aren't something they always consider. It's easy to be wise, after the fact. Hindsight's a wonderful thing.''

''So is foresight.'' He swung around and started retracing their steps. ''I wish I could subscribe to your dewy-eyed belief that love conquers all, Anne-Marie, but the plain fact is, it doesn't. It's fragile and, in the romantic sense at least, short-lived.''

''Are you saying you don't believe in marriage?''

''No. I'm saying it's up to a man to choose wisely. I didn't, and Adrian is still paying the price.''

She was silent for so long that he thought—*hoped*—the topic had exhausted itself. He lived with the knowledge of his own culpability every day. Rehashing it all with this woman, who stirred up emotions and desires best left sleeping, merely added another wrinkle to an already messy situation. He didn't need it. He didn't need her.

But when had she ever been satisfied to let someone else have the last word? ''So if you had everything to do over again,'' she began, the minute they were in the car and headed back to the estate, ''what would you do differently?''

''That's easy,'' he said promptly. ''Choose a woman with Bellefleur blood flowing through her veins—someone born and bred to the rhythm and tempo of this island— instead of settling for an outsider.''

CHAPTER EIGHT

THE second the convertible cruised to a stop in the forecourt, Morton, the butler, came out to meet them, his face creased with worry. "Thank goodness you're home at last, *Monsieur!* I'm afraid there's been an accident. *Madame* Josephine took a bad fall just before lunch."

"Good God! Why wasn't I informed sooner?"

Just how significant a matriarchal role Josephine played showed in the alacrity with which Ethan leaped out of the car while the engine was still running, and in the staccato burst of alarm in his voice as he fired off his question. Equally concerned, Anne-Marie reached across to turn off the ignition, then hurried after the two men as they strode into the house.

"We tried to reach you at the club, but you'd already left, *Monsieur,*" Morton was explaining, when she caught up, "and we were unable to contact you on your cell phone."

Ethan slapped the heel of his hand to his forehead. "I forgot to take the damn thing with me when I went out, that's why. Has the doctor seen her?"

"*Oui, Monsieur.*"

"And? Does my aunt require hospitalization?"

"*Madame* refused to entertain the idea and Doctor Evert agreed she could recuperate at home. She's resting comfortably now, and asked that you and *Mademoiselle* Barclay stop by her room as soon as you returned. She's quite agitated, I'm afraid, and *Monsieur Louis* is beside himself with worry."

"I can imagine," Ethan said grimly. "We'll go up right away." Already halfway across the inner courtyard to the curving staircase at the other end, he crooked a peremptory finger at Anne-Marie. "Follow me."

He'd already taken the bloom off her day with his remark about never entrusting his heart to anyone but an island woman, and that he was now flinging orders at her without so much as a *please* would ordinarily have been enough for her to remind him in no uncertain terms that she was not one of his lackeys.

In this instance, though, Josephine's condition took precedence over Ethan Beaumont's manners, or lack thereof. Still, Anne-Marie couldn't suppress a twinge of regret that the intimacy they'd shared on their stroll through town had lasted such a brief time.

A central hall lined with many closed doors ran the length of the upper floor of the house, with tall, open windows at each end and numerous ceiling fans whirling lazily to keep the air circulating. On the walls between the doors hung portraits of dark-haired, noble-looking men and finely-featured women. Beaumont ancestors, she guessed, glancing at them as she sped by; the resemblance was unmistakable.

The Duclos's suite of rooms lay in a wing at the far end of the house and, as Anne-Marie might have expected, was a spacious, elegant affair with a sitting room, small private dining room and study, all opening onto the usual deep shaded verandahs overlooking a fabulous view down the hillside to the sea.

A shaken Louis ushered them into a bedroom furnished in shades of blue and ivory. Josephine, wearing a froth of beribboned lace and satin, sat propped up on a bank of silk-covered pillows like an aging Cleopatra about to set sail in her barge.

"This is not how I planned to spend the next several days," she proclaimed, waving aside her husband's anxious hovering and patting the edge of the bed in invitation for Anne-Marie to sit. "I've twisted my ankle rather badly, and I'm afraid it's going to create a serious inconvenience, in light of all the entertaining we're facing in the coming days."

"Never mind all that. We'll manage somehow." Ethan glowered affectionately at her from the foot of the bed. "More to the point, how come you fell in the first place? I suppose you were in your usual hurry and not looking where you were going?"

"Don't blame me!" she snapped. "It was that benighted kitten's fault. Ever since Adrian took a shine to it, it's forever underfoot. It's a miracle I didn't break my neck."

His scowl melted into an unabashed grin. "You're an indestructible old woman, *ma tante,* and I don't know why we're wasting sympathy on you. If anyone needs comfort, it's probably the cat."

"The cat," she assured him irascibly, "is perfectly fine, and you have bigger problems to face than worrying about it. Or have you forgotten that the French Trade Envoy and his entourage are joining us for dinner tonight, and staying over until tomorrow?"

"Oh, hell! Yes, I had."

"I expected as much. Well, lucky for you that Anne-Marie is able to take my place as hostess, or you'd be left to cope single-handedly with *Monsieur* Pelletier and that insatiable wife of his."

"Me?" Anne-Marie said. "Oh, surely not! Surely Solange is the one who should take your place?"

"Good heavens, child!" Josephine snorted. "Solange and Philippe are too wrapped up in each other to spare a thought for anyone else. Why, the Envoy could choke on a fish bone and fall face first in his plate, and they wouldn't notice! No, you're the only possible choice.''

"I'm afraid my aunt's right,'' Ethan said. "Solange isn't up to the task, not these days. Too caught up in wedding fever.''

"Precisely.'' Josephine smiled, gracious in victory. "And now that we're all in agreement, Ethan, have Louis show you out. I believe the cook wants your approval on some last-minute changes in the menu. No, my dear, not you,'' she added, when Anne-Marie rose to leave also. "You stay and keep me company a little longer.''

Before leaving, Ethan rested his hand on Anne-Marie's shoulder; a passing touch only, but as always where he was concerned, it stirred up an aftermath of sensation out of all proportion to the occasion. "Will you come up to the house half an hour earlier than usual, Anne-Marie, so that we may greet our guests together?''

"Yes,'' she managed, more elated than she had any right to be at the idea of being his consort for the evening.

"I should warn you, it'll be a somewhat more formal occasion than usual.''

"*More* formal than usual?'' She blinked, taken aback. "I have a hard time imagining how, since everyone here always dresses for dinner.''

"When it's just family, we make an occasion of it, yes, but not to the degree that Mimi Pelletier expects. She shows up looking as if she's about to be presented to the crowned heads of Europe. Full length evening dress, enough jewelry to set up shop, and all that sort of thing. It'll be a long and rather tedious evening, I'm afraid. Are you sure you're up to it?''

"I'll manage,'' she said, her gaze trapped helplessly in his.

"You have something suitable to wear? If not, I'm sure Solange—"

"I have something. Don't worry, Ethan, I won't embarrass you."

"Having never seen you look anything but lovely, it never occurred to me that you might. I was thinking only of how you'd feel if you found you were under-dressed for the occasion."

"I appreciate your concern," she said, drawn ever deeper into the beguiling depths of his blue, blue eyes.

He rewarded her with one of his rare and charming smiles. "Until later, then."

She watched as he dropped a kiss on his aunt's cheek, then followed Louis from the room. The door clicked shut behind them, and left behind a hanging silence marked only by the discreet tick of the exquisite ormolu clock on the bedside table.

At length, Josephine said quietly, "Your face is a picture, child. Everything you're feeling is written there and what I see at this moment is utter turmoil. Is my nephew the reason for it?"

"Yes," she said simply. "He's...different from other men I've known."

"In other words, you don't understand him."

"I don't understand myself, Madame Duclos!"

"Because you're hopelessly attracted to someone who's working so hard to keep you at arm's length?"

"Crazy, isn't it?" Anne-Marie attempted a laugh which fell sadly short of the mark.

"Not really, my dear. Sex has you by the throat, and that tends to befuddle one's faculties."

Appalled, Anne-Marie exclaimed, "Ethan and I haven't had sex!"

"But you've thought about it. Indeed, that's almost *all* you can think about where he's concerned."

"Is it so obvious?" she muttered, burning with embarrassment.

Josephine laughed, not unkindly. "There's no need to look so ashamed. It's mostly about sex at this stage of a relationship, and that's as it should be. Sex is crucial to love between a man and a woman. It's a gift beyond price, and it's meant to be enjoyed. *I* enjoy it. Louis is a magnificent lover! There, does that shock you?"

"In all truth, yes. But not in the way you might think. I just never expected you and I would ever have such a frank discussion."

"We are women, Anne-Marie. It is part of our nature to confide in one another in matters of the heart." She laughed again, a little wickedly this time. "Men are dismayed by that, of course. They don't care for the fact that we...what is that American expression which puts is so well? *Gang up* on them."

By then as curious as she was mortified, Anne-Marie said, "Is that what we're doing? Ganging up on Ethan?"

"Possibly."

"He'd be furious, if he knew."

"He won't hear about it from me." Josephine stroked the fine cotton sheet covering her and sighed. "Ethan is very good at orchestrating other people's lives, but he's in danger of making a terrible mess of his own. And that's why I'm speaking to you so bluntly—because from what I've observed, you might be the one woman to change all that. So the question now becomes, what else can you bring to the relationship, apart from the obvious sexual attraction?"

"At this point, I'm not sure we even have a relationship!"

"Well, the potential for one is certainly there. I'm neither blind nor stupid. I know what to look for. He drives you pleasantly crazy. You can't think straight when he's near. He fills your mind, your heart, your soul. You crave him, even as you fear him, because he threatens to turn your world upside-down. But Ethan will run in the opposite direction if he believes you're drawn to him only because he's beautiful."

"Oh, there's more to it than that!" Anne-Marie protested. "But he's a complicated man. Overcoming the barriers he throws up isn't easy."

"If you can bring yourself to understand what makes him the man he is today, you might find it worth the effort. His experience has been that women can't distinguish between love and infatuation—that they value things like money and prestige and appearances, over unwavering devotion, integrity and, yes, passion. Passion not just for him but for his family, and for the people of this island."

"All the things his ex-wife lacked, in other words."

"Precisely. And once you recognize that, your options become very clear-cut. He'll probably have sex with you, if that's all you want and don't mind walking away without regret afterward. But he'll never again compromise Adrian's happiness, or his own, by allowing himself to fall in love with you, unless you can convince him that you're as capable of loyal commitment as he is."

"That kind of thing takes time—more than I can afford. Once the wedding's over, I'll be gone from here."

"Then make the most of every minute you have left."

"But how, on such short acquaintance, does a person tell the difference between infatuation and love?"

"*Mon Dieu,* child, I don't have *all* the answers! I know only what I see, and bring to those observations only the wisdom of my years. Perhaps what exists between the two of you will never amount to more than a superficial attraction and that, indeed, only time will tell. However, if you sincerely wish to begin the journey of discovery, then for heaven's sake get on with it! Start showing him that you're not someone to be easily dismissed, regardless of where you'll be living a week or two from now! Dare to reveal to him all that's in your heart.''

But did she have that kind of courage? The question plagued Anne-Marie for the rest of the afternoon and throughout the time it took her to dress for dinner.

It was almost midnight, yet the air remained as heavy and close as if the sun still cast its powerful light over the gardens. Exchanging her elegant navy dinner gown for a short sarong printed with scarlet hibiscus, Anne-Marie slipped quietly out of her villa and headed for her favorite retreat.

Though shrouded on either side by deep shadows, the hillside steps lay clearly defined in the moonlight and the sand, when at last she reached the beach and took off her shoes, sifted between her toes like warm flour.

The evening had been a triumph from the moment she set foot in the main house and found Ethan waiting for her. That he'd said not a word when he stepped forward to greet her hadn't mattered. The firm, almost possessive touch of his hand in the small of her back as he guided her into the salon, and the unspoken approval in his eyes as he poured champagne and regarded her over the rim of his glass, had been enough.

It wasn't enough now, though. Everyone else might be so sated with good food, wine and conversation that all they wanted was to flop into bed and sleep off the meal, but she was filled with a restless sense of unfinished business, of anticlimax.

The night should not have ended as it had, with formal handshakes, Gallic air-kissing on both cheeks, and her slipping quietly away in a rustle of midnight silk while Ethan directed the Pelletiers to their overnight accommodation.

There should have been something more exciting to round off the occasion, just as the thimble-sized glasses of fine orange liqueur served with rich island coffee had completed the magnificent dinner.

Maybe that was why she cast aside her usual caution and ventured into the sea. Not far at first, to be sure; just enough for the gentle tide to ebb and flow idly around her calves. Stooping, she swished her hands back and forth, and sent tiny sparks of phosphorescence shooting through the water.

Magical, she thought. *As magical as this night was meant to be.* And made bold by the benign pleasure of the moment, she raised the hem of her sarong and waded in deeper until the waves caressed her thighs as sensually as a lover's hands.

"Oh, Ethan…!" She murmured his name on a tiny breath full of longing which only she could hear.

Or so she thought. But scarcely had the words escaped her than, with blood-chilling suddenness, a hand slid under her hair and closed around the back of her neck. Letting out a muffled shriek of terror, she spun around to find him standing behind her, with the waves lapping at the hem of his khaki shorts.

"For someone who claims to be afraid of anything deeper than a glass of water, you're taking a hell of a chance wading in the shallows at this time of night," he chided. "There are dangers out here, and not all of them lie below the tide line."

"You mean, I could be mugged and robbed?" She pressed a fist to her ribs, to try to settle her erratic heart, and managed a laugh. "I doubt it! I don't have anything on me worth stealing."

His eyes were inscrutable in the dark, his expression unreadable. But his touch, as he trailed his fingers up her throat to her mouth, betrayed a hunger in him which electrified her. "I disagree," he said, his voice deep and dark. "You possess something any man in his right mind would covet."

"I do?" She trembled on the edge of expectancy, sure he would kiss her, and hoping it wouldn't be enough, that he'd want more. That he'd want everything she longed to give.

He didn't—but why should that surprise her? He seldom did what she hoped or expected. He merely led her to the brink of anticipation, and left her dangling there, hungrier than ever.

"You surprised me tonight," he remarked, directing her back to shore. "I knew you spoke some French, but I had no idea you were so fluent in the language, or so conversant with current affairs as they pertain to these islands in general, and to Bellefleur in particular. Pelletier was quite smitten by you."

And you, Ethan? she yearned to ask. *Did I misinterpret the warmth in your gaze at dinner? Was there a reason you glanced at me so often, and always with a hint of a smile playing over your mouth, as if we shared a secret too deeply personal to admit to anyone else?* "His wife was charming, too, but very quiet."

Ethan's laughter echoed across the water. "His wife likes attention—her husband's and that of every other man in the room, but she found slim pickings tonight. You stole the show. Why didn't you tell me how accomplished you are?"

"Why didn't you ask, instead of presuming I'd be an embarrassment to you?"

"I didn't say that, Anne-Marie."

"Perhaps not, but I can read what's going on in your mind."

"Can you really?" he murmured, his voice a smoky, sultry counterpoint to the cadence of the sea. "In that case, this shouldn't come as too much of a surprise."

And then, when she *wasn't* expecting it, he *did* kiss her, bringing his lips to hers in a fierce, erotic invasion of heat which sent her senses swimming. He explored her mouth, and when he knew it as thoroughly as he knew his own, went on with thrilling dedication to discover her throat, her ear, the bare slope of her shoulder.

"I have wanted to do this all night," he said roughly, his hands skimming the length of her spine to her hips, and pulling her so close she could feel the urgent throb of his erection through the layers of his clothing.

She clutched at his upper arms, dazed. How was it possible that, with the simple brush of his lips over her skin, he could reach a place within her unfettered by physical boundaries? By what divine intervention did he know how to touch her soul?

His fingers toyed with the top of her sarong. Dipped into her cleavage with tormenting finesse. A moment later, the fabric whispered down her body and left her breasts bare to his gaze.

"From the moment you appeared on the terrace, right through that interminable dinner and all the civilized conversation that went with it, the only thing I wanted was to get you alone and rip that incredibly sexy gown from your body," he said hoarsely, grazing his palms lightly over her nipples. "Thank God you saved me the trouble. It would have been a pity to lay waste to such a lovely garment."

A spasm of pleasure shot through her and left her skin puckered with sensation. "I didn't realize you felt that way," she whispered. "You seemed so much in command."

He ripped off his shirt. Wrenched open the buckle at his waist, and kicked off the rest of his clothing. Moonlight glimmered over him, painting his bronzed limbs with silver, and she thought that Josephine had said it best: he *was* beautiful.

He took her hand, and placed it against his chest, right over his heart. "Does this feel to you like a man in command?" he rumbled, and when she shook her head in mute denial, drew her fingers lower and boldly closed them around his penis. "Does this?"

Her breathing, shallow enough to begin with, seized up altogether at the power and vitality of him. She felt the strength seep from her legs, the warm, damp heat surge between her thighs. Her knees buckled, and she sank to the sand.

He knelt above her and traced the shape of her from head to toe, his hands warm and possessive. He murmured her name and made it sound like angels singing.

He removed her panties, and parted her legs. Touched her—a single brush of his finger only, but it was enough. Enough to make her cry out in exquisite agony and reach for him, desperate to verify that this was no dream; that he really hovered over her, all lean and hard and ready.

He let her touch him. Thrust himself, hot and smooth, against the curve of her palm, before retreating far enough for a whisper of ocean breeze to flutter over her naked body.

"No...!" she begged on a long sigh. "Come to me, Ethan...please! Come now!"

"All in good time, my lovely *Canadienne*," he murmured hoarsely, touching her again, this time with his mouth…and its talent defied mortal boundaries.

He made her shimmer from the inside out. His tongue delved and stroked, until she arched like a bow, and flew like an arrow. Until she shattered into a million shining fragments, and came together again more alive than she'd ever been before.

He left her begging and pleading and clutching at him. Reaching for him. Wanting more. Wanting *all* of him— everything he ever was or ever would be. And when he finally ended the glorious torment and drove into her, she knew that she'd never again be complete without him.

She closed around him, tight and sleek as a second skin. Contracted around the powerful length of him. And briefly reveled in the hot, sweet rush of his seed flooding into her before, once again, she splintered on another wave of ecstasy.

Of course, it had to end, unrehearsed miracle that their coming together had been, and she braced herself, expecting that, once the rush subsided, he'd pull away and again disappear behind the cool reserve that was too often his stock in trade.

When he did not, and instead lay with his weight pressing her into the soft white sand, and his breath gusting damp at her ear, and his hand idly stroking her hair, a slender hope sprang alive that perhaps he'd been taken by the same emotional storm as she had. Was it possible, she wondered dreamily, that they'd embarked on that journey of discovery Josephine had talked about?

At last—too soon—he stirred and, lifting his head, planted a kiss on the corner of her mouth. "Well?" he said. "How do you feel? Full of regret?"

"Mm-mm." She shook her head, loving the feel of his cheek rasping slightly against hers. "Blissed out! What just happened between us...it was so much more than I dared to hope for!''

Laughter rumbled deep in his chest. ''I'm not sure that's a compliment!''

''Oh, Ethan, never doubt for a moment that it was wonderful!''

''Oui.'' He kissed her again, lightly, tenderly. ''For once, you and I are in agreement. What a pity that it has to end so soon, that we can't spend the rest of this singular night together. But my son—''

''I understand,'' she said. ''You have to be there when Adrian wakes in the morning.''

''Yes.'' He ran his finger over her mouth, unaware of the surge of desire to which his casual embrace gave rise. ''And you, too, must leave, Anne-Marie, because I meant what I said earlier. This is not a smart idea, to be wandering alone in such an isolated spot.''

''But I love it here,'' she reasoned. ''I love to watch the shooting stars streaming across the sky, and the reflection of the moon rippling over the night-calm sea. I love the tranquility of the island at rest, soothed by the quiet lullaby of the surf.''

''Very lyrical, I'm sure, but don't be fooled by it,'' he replied, unmoved. ''The sea can turn into a monster without warning, and who do you think would hear your cries for help and come to your rescue, should you find yourself in difficulties?''

''You,'' she said, leaning into him. ''If there's one thing I've learned since I came here, it's that you're always there when you're needed.''

''Not always. I'm as fallible as the next man, Anne-Marie. You can count on me for only so much.''

It was as close to a warning as she wanted to get, that she shouldn't expect one night to translate into forever.

"Then I'll be more careful," she said lightly. "I'll only ever come here again after dark if I know I won't be alone."

"Temptress!" He smiled, sprang lithely to his feet, and offered his hand. "Come. I'll take you home."

"No." She shook her head, aware that if she presumed too much, pushed too hard for a closeness he wasn't ready to accept, then the regrets he'd spoken of would arise, and they'd be all his. "I can make it back on my own. I've traveled the cliff path often enough in the dark that I'm familiar with it."

"But I have another way, safer and swifter." He gestured down the beach to a spot where the encroaching jungle met the sand in a tangle of lush undergrowth, and she saw a horse grazing there; a ghostly, graceful creature, its flanks dappled by moonlight. So that was how he'd managed to sneak up on her so easily!

"Come," he said again, climbing into his clothes and draping her sarong around her breasts. "This way, we can prolong the pleasure of the night a little longer."

Denying him was beyond her. He vaulted astride the animal, then reached down and hoisted her up behind him. "Hold on tight," he ordered—as if she needed any encouragement!—clicked his tongue, and they were off in a powdery thud of hooves, a mile or more along the shore to a place where a broad trail opened out.

She'd never ridden bareback before; never clung to a body so lean and strong and capable; never felt so secure, so cherished. And she knew that if she lived to be a hundred, the memory of this night would remain, undimmed by the passing years.

It ended too soon, of course. Cresting a final slope, Ethan drew the horse to a halt in the lee of guest pavilions, and dismounted. "*À demain, ma chère,*" he murmured, as she slid down into his waiting arms. "Sleep well."

À demain—until tomorrow.

Oh, yes, she'd sleep! And with such implicit promise to pave the way, in her dreams she'd hoard every touch, every kiss, every word they'd exchanged. "*Oui,*" she breathed, lifting her face for one last kiss. "*À demain.*"

CHAPTER NINE

SHE did indeed see Ethan the next morning, but only from a distance. Since he appeared to be in a hurry and too preoccupied to notice her, she didn't attempt to draw his attention. Refusing to allow the keen sense of letdown to take hold—for what woman wanted to learn that she was so soon forgettable?—she instead took herself back to her workroom, and told herself to stop behaving like a teenager in the throes of puppy love. One encounter, no matter how memorable, did not amount to a lifetime commitment, except in romance novels.

Later that afternoon though, when she stopped by to visit Josephine, and learned that he and Adrian had flown to Miami and would be gone at least overnight and possibly longer, her disappointment wasn't so easy to contain.

"Did he not bother to tell you he was called away?" Josephine inquired, skewering Anne-Marie in her penetrating, all-seeing gaze, and discerning far too much.

"Why would he?" Anne-Marie looked out at the blue afternoon with pretended indifference. So much for making an indelible impression on the man! "He hardly needs my permission to go wherever he pleases."

For the next forty-eight hours, she put aside her dented pride and drove herself to the point of exhaustion, finishing the dresses. But best intentions notwithstanding, nothing could silence the questions hammering in her head. *Why hadn't Ethan told her he was leaving? Was he deliberately avoiding her? Was this his way of telling her that, in the greater scheme of things, she simply didn't count?*

It didn't help any that the heat grew intolerable. Heavy as a wet cloth pressed to one's face, it sapped both her energy and her normally sunny disposition.

"You're awfully crabby," Solange remarked, toward the end of the second day.

"You would be, too, if you were shackled to a sewing **machi**ne for fifteen hours at a stretch in weather like this!" she snapped.

Solange flinched. "Oh, you're working too hard, and it's all my fault. I shouldn't have imposed on you like this."

Ashamed, because she knew how brittle her friend's self-esteem was, Anne-Marie took as deep a breath as the humidity would allow, and said apologetically, "It's no one's fault but my own, Solange, and I had no business taking my frustrations out on you."

Nor had she. She was twenty-eight years old, and if she didn't have a string of past lovers to draw on for comparison, she'd at least been around long enough to know that impulsive one-night stands seldom amounted to anything permanent. Never mind that Ethan had said and done all the right things after the fact. He was too much the gentleman to behave otherwise.

That evening, the clouds swept in from the east, dark and threatening. Rather than get caught in a downpour, she and Solange had an early dinner delivered to their quarters. By eight o'clock, lightning split the night sky, and thunder rolled down the hillside. A gale rattled the palm tree fronds and tore blossoms from the shrubs bordering the little terrace. Shortly after, the lights went out.

"Power failures happen regularly during stormy weather," Solange told her, lighting candles. "It's the one drawback to living here. But candlelight's so romantic, don't you think?"

"For you, perhaps," Anne-Marie said, and took herself off to her own rooms, there to lie alone in a bed large enough for two, but with only the filmy mosquito netting for company.

She awoke the next morning to tranquil skies, calm seas and the overwhelming scent of freshly washed flowers. Bellefleur was living up to its name in fine style.

Refreshed herself, for the storm had cleared her mind as well as the air, she hung the finished gowns in garment bags and supervised their shipping to the main house, for storage until the big day. After seeing them safely stowed in an empty dressing room, she came back along the upper hall to find Ethan waiting for her at the foot of the stairs.

"I hear you've been busy," he said, his glance sweeping over her as she descended to the main floor.

"I hear you've been away," she shot back, and could have slapped herself for sounding so piqued.

His lips twitched. "Did you miss us, Anne-Marie?"

"I missed Adrian," she said scornfully. "But you? I barely noticed you were gone."

The twitch became a full-blown grin. "We missed you, too."

"Sure you did," she said, hanging on to her annoyance because it was her only defense against such an onslaught of charm. "And the little pigs of Bellefleur have wings, and fly."

He pressed his lips together, but although that contained his laughter, it did nothing to quell the amusement dancing in his eyes. "There are no pigs on Bellefleur, *Chérie*. Only sheep, horses and cattle. Oh yes, and a little boy who's learning to sail, and panting to have you come and applaud his progress." He caught her hand and drew her down the last two stairs. "And now that you're finally done with the wedding gowns, you have no reason to refuse him."

Resolve growing weaker by the second, she muttered, "I suppose not."

"Excellent! Perhaps you'd like to try handling a small boat yourself?"

"I'm not prepared to go quite that far," she said, turned weak at the knees by the warmth in his eyes when he looked at her, "but I'd love to see how Adrian manages."

They went to a different beach, one she hadn't visited before, with a boathouse, and a launching ramp. After strapping a life jacket on Adrian, Ethan released a small, low-slung, lateen-rigged boat down the ramp into the water.

"Sure you don't want to come with us?" he asked her, as his son dog-paddled after him and climbed into the shallow cockpit. "There's room for three, an extra life preserver on board, and we're not going out more than a couple of hundred yards."

"I'm sure," she said, chilled despite the warmth of the sun, at the thought of being out of her depth on such a flimsy craft.

"I won't let you drown, I promise. You're too important to Solange for me to take chances with your safety."

"Only to Solange?" she mocked, hearing the teasing note in his voice.

"Not only to Solange," he said. "To me, and to my son."

They were words she lived to hear, but even they couldn't persuade her to climb aboard that frail-looking little dingy. So she lifted the camera slung around her neck and said, "Go give your son his lesson, then. I'm happy to be the official photographer."

And so the remaining days spun out, with her accompanying them when they went sailing, or swimming off the beach. And willingly, foolishly, she let herself slip into a surrogate mother role, making sure Adrian wore sunscreen and a hat, and wrapping him in a towel to dry him off when he fell overboard.

She was the one he ran to for comfort when he scraped his knee on a chunk of coral. And hers was the heart he melted when he wound his little arms around her neck and told her she was pretty, and that he loved her and didn't want her to go away, not ever.

The nights followed a different theme, one of secret, searing passion between adults. With long hours stretching ahead and nothing to distract them from each other, Ethan came to her, sometimes on the beach, under a full, benevolent moon, and sometimes in her villa.

Yet at some level, she knew that he did so with a reluctance outpaced only by his raging hunger; that he wished he could rise above such carnal needs. Sometimes, she suspected he hated himself for wanting her so much, and even though, deep down, instinct told her that such self-loathing could lash out and direct itself at her, she didn't care. He swept her into a world so deeply, thrillingly sexual that she lost her sense of survival, and lived only for the pleasure of the hours they shared.

To touch him, to taste him, and to know that with her mouth and hands she could smash through his formidable reserve and connect with him at the most intimate, elemental level, became, during those star-filled nights, her *raison d'être*.

She lived for his kiss. Died a tiny death every time he brought her to orgasm. And, responsive to his slightest touch, was born again within minutes.

When foreplay tore his self-control to shreds, she loved the feel of him entering her. She loved the power and thrust of his manhood; his stamina and strength. She gloried in hearing him groan helplessly against her mouth as she teased his flesh; in feeling the muscles of his belly flex like tempered steel as he cajoled her to yet another climax while fighting to delay his own.

She loved the battle, the way the balance of power shifted between them. Relished her fleeting little victories. But in the end, he always won, hurling her beyond the limits of mortal endurance in a shattering explosion of sensation and release. After, she clung to him, sometimes weeping from the intensity of the experience, and always amazed that she'd survived so wrenching an emotional catharsis.

But unlike his son, Ethan always withheld a part of himself. He never begged her not to leave the island. Never, no matter how rich or full the passion between them, forgot himself so far as to tell her he loved her. And if part of her brain warned her that she was a temporary diversion only and was setting herself up for heartbreak by pretending otherwise, another, larger part refused to listen.

Today was all that mattered. And if she made it matter enough to Ethan, perhaps tomorrow would never come.

Sadly, though, it did, and so abruptly that she was caught completely unprepared.

"I'm afraid this is the last time we'll be able to spend the afternoon fooling around like this," he announced, hauling the boat into its covered berth, the Saturday before the wedding. "The first of the off-island guests arrive tomorrow, which means my time won't be my own between now and the day itself. Nor, come to that, will yours, seeing that my aunt still isn't up to par."

Although not a cloud marred the perfection of the sky, suddenly the sea appeared less blue, the sun not quite as bright. Unable to hide her dismay, she said, "Why so soon? The wedding's still a week away!"

"True, and most people won't arrive until a day or two

before. But for close friends flying in from halfway around the world, it's the chance to visit before the event, and make a holiday of it. We'll have a full house by Monday, with more arriving daily.''

''If the main house is full, where will the rest of them stay?''

''Some will take rooms at the Plantation Club, and others will stay with friends who live here year-round. It'll be a bit of a squeeze, fitting everyone in, but we'll manage somehow.''

''You must be wishing I wasn't taking up an entire guest villa all to myself,'' she said, hoping he'd take her not-so-subtle hint and rush to assure her that he liked her living arrangements just as they were because, that way, they could continue their midnight trysts undetected.

Instead, he replied, ''In light of everything you've done to help out, you've more than earned the right to a little extra comfort. We're all very grateful to you, Anne-Marie.''

Grateful: the word assaulted her, sharper than a blade sliding between her ribs to rip open her heart.

''And is that what these last days all come down to, Ethan?'' she cried, detesting the shrill edge in her voice, but helpless to control it. ''You're *grateful?*''

''Of course. You've been wonderful, stepping in whenever we've needed you. What else did you expect—that we'd simply take you for granted?''

Thoroughly deflated, she said, ''No.''

''But you're upset.''

'''Upset' doesn't begin to cover it, but how like a man to understate matters!''

''And how like a woman to take exception to a perfectly innocuous remark,'' he said, casting a pointed glance at

Adrian who, although he didn't fully grasp the gist of the conversation, clearly picked up on the tension underlying it.

Filled with remorse at the confusion and fear she saw printed on the child's face, she said, "You're quite right. I don't know what possessed me to overreact like that. All I can say is that, for months, I've looked forward to seeing Solange and Philippe get married, but now that the time's here, I'm almost sorry."

"Why is that? Are you having second thoughts about their chances of making it work?"

"No, not that." She drummed up a smile, even though the effort made her face ache. "I suppose, if truth be told, I'd like things to remain the same as they've been for the last little while."

It was as close as she dared come to admitting outright all that was in her heart, but it didn't elicit a similar response from Ethan. "Nothing stays the same forever, Anne-Marie," he said, averting his eyes. "We've both known that from the beginning."

Just to hammer home the message, life as she knew it at the Beaumont estate underwent dramatic change from that point on. With the growing influx of international guests, lunches became more formal, dinners more elaborate, and the social calendar more crowded.

If they weren't out sailing, or riding horses, or playing croquet, or a round of golf, the visitors lolled around the pool, a sophisticated crowd of jet-setters whose unflagging amiability set Anne-Marie's teeth on edge.

"Thanks," she said, when Ethan urged her to join in the fun while it lasted, "but I suspect Adrian's feeling a little neglected, so if it's all the same to you, I'll spend some time with him instead."

''That's very thoughtful of you,'' he replied.

Oh, that's me, all right! she thought bitterly. *Thoughtful, helpful—and stupid to a fault for falling in love with a man who's not the least bit interested in a permanent addition to his household.*

For distraction, she turned again to work, more than happy to go along with Adrian's request that she make him something special to wear at the wedding ''because I'm carrying the rings and that's important,'' he said.

''Tell me what you'd like, then,'' she said.

''A space suit,'' he replied promptly. ''A silver one, with a helmet.''

''Okay, let's see what I come up with.''

Fifteen minutes later, she submitted three drawings for his approval. ''That one,'' he decided, selecting a Pierrot-style jumpsuit with flared legs and ruffled collar.

''That's my favorite, too,'' she said, hugging him.

The next morning, they went into town, to a little shop on the waterfront, and chose a length of fine white fabric in a silk-linen blend with just enough shine to it that it might have passed for silver if a person used his imagination. Afterward, they stood at a booth in the market and ate crayfish sandwiches, before climbing in the Mercedes and being driven back to the estate.

He was such a delight, and so happy to have her shower him with attention. Every morning, he'd show up at her door, and stand patiently while she measured and fitted the garment.

''You'll be the best-dressed man there,'' she told him, fashioning the underside of the ruffled collar from a scrap of turquoise silk left over from the bridesmaid's dresses. ''Every lady will want to dance with you at the reception.''

But, ''I'm only going to dance with you,'' he said.

"You're my favorite lady in all the world. I love you, Anne-Marie."

"Oh, darling!" She sighed, her heart breaking for him, that he'd latched onto her, a stranger, when his mother should have been the recipient of his affection. "I love you, too."

Something of her own unhappiness must have shown in her voice because, after looking at her from his big, dark eyes a moment, he observed with preternatural insight, "Loving people is scary sometimes, isn't it? Sometimes, it's better not to, then you don't get sad if they don't love you back, but you can't always help it, can you?"

Dear God! she thought. *That a child so young should have learned such a painful lesson already is nothing short of criminal!*

If she could have, she'd have kept them both down at the guest villa, and stayed away from the main house altogether. She'd have hoarded every second of the time the time she had left on that magical island, and lavished him with all the love she had to give. That, though, wasn't an option.

"You need a little adult conversation once in a while, and Ethan still needs a hostess," Josephine informed her, catching her one day when she stopped by the main house on an errand for Solange. "I can do my part at lunch, but I'm too old to stay up half the night, smiling at people whose names I can't remember, and laughing at jokes I don't understand. You'll have to fill in for me, child, and that's all there is to it."

Of course, Anne-Marie agreed, but it was difficult to preserve a serene facade when she went hot all over every time Ethan looked at her, and every time she looked at him. To be so close and not be allowed to touch, made her ache. And for all his apparent willingness to let their affair lapse, there were times, when some other man in the party perhaps drank a little too much champagne and paid her too much attention, that she thought she detected in Ethan's eyes a proprietary interest that amounted almost to jealousy.

Was this how the rest of her time on Bellefleur was destined to play itself out? she wondered, as the week progressed. With her teetering on the edge of despair, and him alternating between bland indifference and covert possessiveness?

On the Thursday before the pre-wedding party at the Tourneaus, she got her answer. Pleading fatigue, she'd excused herself shortly after dinner, and was on her way out of the salon when Ethan caught up with her and murmured simply, "Later?"

Her weariness evaporated in a flash, replaced by such exhilaration that she didn't know how she remained earthbound. "Later," she breathed, her spirits soaring, and sped back to the guest villa on winged feet.

He did care, at least a little bit! And a little was better than nothing.

In a haze of euphoria, she took a leisurely bath, knowing the social hour at the main house was far from over and that she had plenty of time in which to make herself pretty for him. She shampooed her hair and rinsed it with rose water. Massaged lightly perfumed body lotion into her sun-kissed skin. Then, wearing nothing but moon shadows for a nightgown, she pulled the mosquito netting around the bed and slipped under the fine cotton sheets, to wait for him.

At last, when the music and laughter no longer drifted on the air, and the estate had sunk into a sleepy silence broken only by the occasional night sound of the jungle, Ethan emerged from the shadows.

It had been six nights since they'd made love and she, it appeared, was not the only one to have suffered from it. With a harsh intake of breath, he crossed the room, flung back the netting surrounding her bed, and reached for her in a frenzy of pent-up desire.

She rose up to meet him, and he buried his mouth against hers in a long, fierce kiss. Ran his hands up her back and down again, as if he were blind and every vertebra, every rib, every delicate muscle and tendon, spoke to him in Braille.

And when that wasn't enough to ease the ache of wanting, he ripped off his clothes and came to her in a driving rhythm so powerful that it rocked the world on its axis. So intimate that it cocooned them in a universe all their own, with neither space nor time nor wish for any other soul to share it with them.

"Mon Dieu," he rasped against her mouth, as the tempo of their loving raced toward a stupendous finale, "what have you done to me, woman, that I'm so bewitched by you?"

She clung to him, desperate to halt the encroaching tremors building within her and prolong the pleasure. She turned her face to his neck and tasted the salt of his sweat as he fought his own demons of desire.

With her legs locked around his waist, she drew him deeper into her, fusing him to her so tightly that there was no discerning where he ended and she began. "I love you, Ethan," she whispered, in thrall to the convulsive pleasure overtaking her. *"I love you!"*

For a moment, he braced himself above her, his eyes wide with shock, his arms so rigid that the tendons quivered in the pale light. Then, with a groan of pure agony, he collapsed against her.

She felt his sudden gush of liquid heat, the powerful

aftershocks which shook them both, and finally, as the world outside swam back into focus, the horrified realization of what she'd said struck home.

The silence which ensued boomed with unbearable suspense and she sought desperately for words to fill it—something sane and uncompromising. Something which would reverse the damage she'd done with her impulsive confession, and return them both to that lovely, intimate place they'd shared, such a short time ago.

Nothing came to mind and, frantic to fill the void, she muttered haltingly, "Have I ruined everything, Ethan?"

He pulled away from her, swung his legs over the side of the bed and combed his fingers through his hair. "You've taken me by surprise," he said.

"Me, too. I had no idea I was going to...say what I did."

"I know. Which is why we both need to sleep on it." He shook his head, as if to clear it of thoughts he didn't want to entertain, and reached for his clothes.

As miserable then, as she'd been transported, mere minutes before, she watched as he pulled on his pants, thrust his arms into the sleeves of his shirt, and tucked the tail in at his waist. That he couldn't be gone soon enough was patently obvious.

Yet, at the last, he stopped at the foot of the bed and said kindly, "Don't look so traumatized, Anne-Marie. You're off the hook. I'm very well aware that you spoke in the heat of the moment, and will wake up in the morning wondering what in the world possessed you."

But as things turned out, she didn't come to that realization quite so soon. Not, in fact, until the following evening.

CHAPTER TEN

"TRULY, these friends of yours know how to throw a party!" Solange's mother, Veronique Fortier, who'd arrived on Bellefleur just that afternoon with her husband, stepped out of the Beaumont limousine in the forecourt of the Tourneau mansion, and surveyed the scene with a condescending approval which, in Anne-Marie's opinion, fell nothing short of insulting. "I confess, we had not expected such glamour and sophistication in so provincial a spot, *n'est-ce pas, mon amour?*"

Monsieur le Consul Maurice Fortier, suave and silver-haired, slipped an arm around his wife's fashionably thin frame and smiled apologetically at Josephine, who was glaring at the mother of the bride with fire in her eyes. How he'd managed to climb so high in the diplomatic corps with a spouse given to such decidedly undiplomatic remarks was something Anne-Marie had never been able to fathom.

"From all I've so far seen, Bellefleur appears to me to be thoroughly charming," he murmured.

In one respect, though, Veronique was quite right. The Tourneaus had spared no expense or trouble to make the evening memorable. Massive bouquets in lacquered jardinieres lined the steps and entrance hall, filled the reception rooms with their exotic perfume, and spilled down the terraces outside to join the profusion of flowers growing in the walled garden to the rear.

In the large, formal salon, a harpist plucked softly at her instrument for the pleasure of those guests seated there and at the small tables on the adjoining terrace. Down on the beach where a younger crowd gathered, the throbbing beat of a steel band filled the night.

Long, linen-draped tables in the dining hall groaned under a selection of Beluga caviar, prawns, smoked Scottish salmon, and Atlantic lobster flown in fresh that morning. A fleet of white-clad servants stood ready to serve guests. Champagne flowed like water.

The place was already crowded when the Beaumont contingent arrived, and for that, Anne-Marie was grateful. The strain of behaving as if nothing untoward had occurred between her and Ethan the previous night was taking a frightful toll, and it didn't help any that social etiquette demanded he act as her escort now.

"Please don't feel you have to stay with me," she said stiffly after, with faultless courtesy, he'd introduced her to the Tourneaus. "I'm sure there are other people here whom you'd rather socialize with, and I'm long past the age where I need a baby-sitter."

He snagged a couple of glasses of champagne from a passing waiter and pressed one into her hand. "Drink this, Anne-Marie," he ordered. "It might help sweeten your mood. And just for the record, I *never* allow myself to be coerced into spending time with someone I'd prefer to avoid."

"Not as a rule, perhaps, but you haven't been left with much of a choice lately, have you? I'm the unattached woman who can't be allowed to feel like a wallflower, and you're the one stuck with the job of keeping me entertained."

He inspected her at leisure, his blue eyes thoughtful as they swept from the top of her blond head to the tips of her strappy little gold sandals, and finally came to rest on the agitated rise and fall of her breasts. "Is that why you think I came to your bed last night?'' he asked mildly. ''To keep you entertained?''

She blushed so deeply, she was sure it was hard to tell where her rose-pink dress ended and her skin began. ''I really haven't given the matter much thought.''

''You're an atrocious liar, *ma chère*. You've thought of little else, and so, come to that, have I.'' He grasped her elbow and held her firmly to his side. ''And I think it's time we spoke frankly to one another about this elephant in the room which no one but the two of us can see.''

''You want to talk about *us* in here?'' She looked around at the crush of people, appalled. ''For heaven's sake, Ethan, I might have spoken out of turn last night, but I don't deserve to be publicly humiliated for it.''

He smiled. ''Of course not *here, Chérie!* We'll find a more private place. Did I mention, by the way, how lovely you look this evening?''

''Flattering me isn't necessary to soften the blow of whatever it is you're about to tell me.''

''What if I'm merely being truthful?'' he said, steering her outside to a quiet corner of the terrace lit only by candles hanging in delicate glass lanterns from the branches of a nearby tree.

Recalling the trouble it had landed her in the night before, she said, ''I'm not sure the truth is always such a good thing.''

''It's the *only* thing that matters between a man and a woman. How can there ever be trust, if there isn't truth?''

More agitated by the second, she twisted the pearl ring on her finger and looked away. ''You're right, of course— about everything. I'm not a good liar, never have been, and the plain truth is, I'm not feeling nearly as brave now as I was last night. In fact, I'm downright panic-stricken.''

''Then let me put you out of your misery,'' he said,

stilling the nervous movement of her hands and raising them to his lips. "You're a beautiful, generous woman, Anne-Marie, and I'd hate to think I'm too blind to recognize a gem when I see one. But—"

Sweet heaven, in trying to let her down gently, he was going to kill her with kindness! "But you're not in love with me," she babbled, unable to bear another tortured moment of uncertainty. "I understand, I really do! For some men, there's only ever one woman, one great love, and yours was your ex-wife."

"Lisa?" He laughed incredulously, and slid his hands up her arms. "Wherever did you get such an idea? She is so far from relevant to this situation that her name is an obscenity."

His touch was firm and sure, his mouth so close that she could practically taste it. For the first time in nearly twenty-four hours, a warmth chased away the chill in her blood and, against all odds, a slender thread of hope wound through her despair. Hardly daring to breathe for fear she'd shatter the mood, she whispered, "What are you saying, Ethan?"

Before he could answer, a group of four men came out of the house and when they caught sight of him, immediately headed his way. Cursing softly, he said, "I'm sorry, Anne-Marie, but it's going to have to wait. These are business associates from Venezuela, here only for a couple of days. There are matters I need to discuss with them, and if I don't do it now, I don't know when another opportunity will present itself. Will you wait for me in the garden until I'm finished?"

She nodded, swept away on a buoyant wave of optimism.

"Thank you, *mon ange.*" Cupping her cheek briefly, tenderly, he gestured to a spot beyond the immediate area.

"Hidden behind that screen of bougainvillea is a stone bench overlooking a small reflecting pool where we can talk without being disturbed. I'll meet you there."

The place was just as he described, quiet and secluded. Sprays of bougainvillea hung down from the trellis, with a few spent blossoms littering the bench which still retained the heat of the day's sun. The silver disc of the moon peeped at its image on the surface of the pool, but threw deep shadows everywhere else. Beyond the wall, the sea rolled ashore in long, lazy sighs.

Deciding she was about as close to paradise as she'd ever expected to find herself, Anne-Marie bent to brush away the papery fallen petals, and was about to sit down when footsteps approached on the other side of the screen.

"I had a wonderful time," a woman's voice, low, sultry, and unpleasantly familiar, was saying. "Miami is my kind of city and Ethan my kind of man. But we'd have had an even better time if he hadn't also brought along that tiresome child of his. I ask you, Roberto, what is the point in having more money than you can spend in four lifetimes, if you don't put it to good use? The boy could very well have been left in the care of the hired servants. Isn't that what they're for?"

"*Sí,*" the man replied, his heavy Spanish accent and the mention of his name enough to clarify in Anne-Marie's mind where she'd seen and heard both him and the woman before.

Roberto Santos and Desirée LaSalle at the Plantation Club, of course!

"Do I take it then," he continued, "that you and Beaumont didn't share the same bed?"

"Alas, no."

"What a waste. The man's a bigger fool than I took him to be."

"But we had adjoining rooms." She laughed. "Once this family wedding is over and he's no longer saddled with playing nursemaid to the bride's little seamstress friend, he and I will pay a return visit to Miami. And I can promise you, Roberto, that when we do, the boy will not be coming with us, nor will there be a door separating us. I'll see to it that *nothing* comes between me and Ethan. Nothing."

"By the bride's little friend, you're referring to the Canadian?"

"Yes. Have you met her?"

"Only briefly. I found her charming."

"Then I wish you the joy of her." Desirée's voice, languid with amusement, faded as they wandered away. "I found her quite pathetic, and so, I suspect, does my poor Ethan. But he's a man of the world. He knows how to make the best of a bad situation and she's apparently very good with the child. As long as the boy's happy, Ethan will put up with a lot—too much, if you ask me! Sometimes, I think he's in danger of forgetting that there's life beyond fatherhood...."

The bench was not warm, Anne-Marie decided, realizing she was gripping its rounded edge as if her life depended on it. It was cold and hard and brutal. It cut into her hand more cruelly than a knife. Her manicure, perfect until a few moments before, was ruined. As for her heart....

She scrunched her eyes shut and drew in a tortured breath. Oh, the bench was not the only thing cast in stone! A chunk the size of her fist lay lodged behind her ribs where her heart used to be, and the pain it caused made her wish she was dead.

But that wasn't a choice. Apart from anything else,

Ethan Beaumont wasn't worth dying for, and if she hadn't known it before, she knew it now. Not only that, she'd see him in a hell to equal hers before she'd sit there in abeyance, waiting for him to show up when it was convenient, armed with more of his double-edged sweet talk!

She stalked back to the terrace, and saw at once that he was still so deep in discussion with his Venezuelan contacts that if she'd fallen in a dead faint at his feet, he probably wouldn't have noticed. Yet for all that she reviled herself for such weakness, she noticed everything about him: the pristine white jacket fitting so snugly across his broad shoulders; his dark handsome head tilted attentively as he listened to his associates; his eyes, turned navy in the candlelight, narrowed in concentration.

He leaned one elbow on the arm of his chair and propped his chin on his fist. Nodded once or twice, then gestured in response to something one of the others said. And remembering with wrenching recall how, the night before, he'd gazed at her with just the same intentness, and laid those long, clever hands on her body, Anne-Marie experienced a bolting ache of despair which made her stagger.

How naive she'd been, to think she'd ever meant anything special to him. Oh, he'd made love to her—or then again, perhaps not. Perhaps he'd merely taken her—and only now did she understand how accurate a term that was. Because he'd stolen her from herself. Robbed her of all the things which once had given her life meaning.

Blindly, she reached out, trying to regain her balance, and felt her hand grasped in a steady masculine grip. "You look pale, *señorita*," Roberto Santos murmured, bending over her. "Does the island heat not agree with you?"

Beads of perspiration broke out on her upper lip, her stomach heaved, and she was horribly afraid she might be sick. "Apparently not," she whispered, at which he slipped his arm around her waist, guided her to an empty table, and pulled out a chair.

"I will find something to revive you," he said.

"You're very kind." She fanned herself with a napkin. "Thank you."

Within seconds he returned, bearing a tall glass of water. Grateful, she accepted it and after a sip or two, rolled the side of the frosted tumbler across her heated forehead.

"Better?" Roberto Santos inquired, taking a seat opposite and watching her from heavy-lidded eyes.

She nodded. "Much. I don't know what came over me so suddenly. The heat has never bothered me before tonight."

"Then perhaps the blame lies elsewhere."

"I'm sure it does," she said, not about to admit anything incriminating which might find its way back to Desirée LaSalle's malicious ears. "I suspect I've been working too hard and not getting out enough."

"Is there anything I can do to remedy that?"

A commotion at the table in the corner caught her attention and, turning her head, she saw that Ethan had noticed both her and her companion. His glare fairly scorched the distance separating them, and he'd started up from his table so abruptly that a glass had fallen and smashed on the floor.

Deliberately turning back to Roberto Santos whose glance had followed hers, she said, "I'm actually feeling much better suddenly. If you'll join me, I'd like a glass of champagne and something to eat, and after that, I think I'd like to dance."

His teeth gleamed in a small, knowing smile. Rising, he offered her his arm. "It will be my pleasure to accommodate you on all counts, *Señorita* Barclay. Shall we go inside?''

''By all means. And let's not stand on ceremony. Please call me Anne-Marie.''

''I shall call you Anna-Maria,'' he murmured, dipping his head to hers until his black ponytail almost brushed her cheek. ''It flows more musically in Spanish, don't you agree?''

''*Sí,*'' she cooed, favoring him with her most dazzling smile, all the time vividly aware of Ethan as she swayed past his table close enough that he could have tripped her up if he'd had the wits to stick his foot out far enough. But he appeared too paralyzed with rage to move.

Fine! Let him stew in his own juice, for a change!

Once inside the house, though, with no Ethan for a captive audience, the game of one-upmanship lost what little charm it possessed. ''I'm really not up to this, after all,'' she said, begging off a third energetic samba with Roberto. ''Would you be kind enough to find *Monsieur* Beaumont's driver and ask him to take me home?''

But it turned out that, not ten minutes earlier, Josephine and Louis had commandeered the chauffeur for the same task. ''Which is no problem at all, Anna-Maria,'' Roberto assured her. ''I'll be happy to drive you there myself.''

She knew that, in accepting, she was courting trouble, but it didn't compare to what she'd already endured that night. If he tried to make a pass at her, she'd set him straight in very short order.

He surprised her, though, making no effort to touch her or engage her in innuendo of any kind. If anything, he seemed genuinely sympathetic, an impression borne out when, before leaving her at the villa gates, he handed her a business card and said, ''If circumstances were otherwise, I would suggest a different way to end this evening.

But I see that you are deeply troubled and so I will say only this: if I can be of service to you in any capacity during the remainder of your stay here, Anna-Maria, you have only to ask. I can be reached at this number anytime, day or night.''

Embarrassed to find herself on the brink of tears, she took the card and said, ''You've already been of enormous help. I don't know how I would have managed tonight, if you hadn't stepped forward to pick up the pieces when I fell apart at the Tourneaus.''

He shrugged. ''I had no choice. I am not a popular figure on Bellefleur as, I'm sure, you're probably aware. I have made mistakes and will likely make many more before I die. But I am not the monster Ethan makes me out to be. I am simply a man who finds it difficult to turn his back on a woman in distress. So I say to you again, if you need me, you have only to call.''

''No,'' she said wearily. ''It wouldn't be fair, and my stay here is almost over anyway. So do yourself a favor and forget this night ever happened, Roberto. I certainly intend to.''

A midnight hush hung over the moon-dappled gardens as she made her way down to her quarters. That such calm beauty reigned all around while nothing but ugliness ate away at her, was more than she could bear. Stripping off her sandals, she ran barefoot the last hundred yards and didn't stop until, out of breath and out of emotional stamina, she gained refuge inside the villa.

''Three more days,'' she mumbled, feeling her way into the bedroom, and slumping against the wall, too weary to undress and climb into bed. ''Three more days, and then I'll be out of here. It can't happen soon enough.''

''I quite agree.'' Ethan's voice swam out of the dark,

startling her so thoroughly that she let out a shriek. And then, before she could begin to regain her composure, he turned on a lamp and, dazzled, she dropped her sandals and flung up her arm to shield her eyes.

"What's the matter, Anne-Marie?" he inquired coldly. "Too ashamed to look me in the face?"

"*Me* ashamed?" she spluttered, squinting to where he slouched in one of the wicker chairs on the verandah. "You've got some nerve, Ethan Beaumont, accusing me of that! And what the hell do you think you're doing, sneaking into my room like this?"

"You've never objected before, my dear. What's the problem, this time? Afraid there won't be room for three of us in the bed?" He hitched himself straighter in the chair and made a big production of craning his neck to scan the open doorway beside her. "Where is Santos, by the way? Lying in the weeds, waiting to be sure the coast is clear before he makes his next move?"

"I won't even dignify that remark with a reply," she informed him, "although I suppose I shouldn't be surprised that you'd try to shift responsibility for this night's fiasco to my shoulders. It's typical behavior for the abuser to heap blame on his victim."

"You're my victim?" He rose smoothly from his seat to loom, tall and dangerous, over her. "Then I must have missed something in your little performance at the Tourneaus, because I'm of a distinctly different impression. Enlighten me, please."

She turned away because, even in his present ugly mood, she was still so drawn to him that all she wanted to do was fling herself into his arms and forget every horrible thing she'd learned in the past few hours. "Just before your business associates showed up tonight, you were about to bare your soul to me, Ethan. What was it you were so anxious to tell me—that you'd taken Desirée LaSalle with you to Miami, perhaps?''

He didn't flinch. "No," he said calmly. "On that subject, there's nothing to tell."

"Oh, please! I overheard her bragging about how you had adjoining rooms."

"Yes? And your point is?"

"That you've been lying to me!" she cried. "You told me you weren't interested in her."

"I'm not."

"So why did you take her with you?"

"She wanted to go shopping. Miami has some very good shops. There are very few commercial flights from here to the mainland. I had space on my private jet. Does that answer your question?"

"She said…." What *had* Desirée LaSalle said, exactly? Pinching the bridge of her nose between two fingers, Anne-Marie shook her head. "She *said*—"

"I really don't care what she said," Ethan said softly. "What concerns me is that you set such store by it. We talked about establishing a bond of trust earlier. If finding out exactly what did or did not take place between me and Desirée was so upsetting to you, why didn't you come to me, instead of turning for comfort to a man like Roberto Santos?"

"If you had nothing to hide, why didn't you tell me of your own free will that she was with you? You've had opportunity enough."

"I am your host, not your husband, Anne-Marie. I neither needed your permission nor owed you an explanation. Furthermore, in case you've forgotten, Adrian also went with me to Miami. I'd hardly expose him to the kind of behavior you're accusing me of, and I thought you knew me better than to suppose I would."

At some level, she recognized both the truth and the logic of what he told her. But that he could remain so unmoved in the face of her obvious distress goaded her to recklessness. "Clearly, I don't know you well at all."

"Nor I, you. What a good thing we've shown ourselves in our true colors, before matters between us progressed further."

"They were never going to progress further, Ethan! Do you think I couldn't see what you were leading up to, tonight? Oh, you were being very gentlemanly, very charming, but it doesn't change the fact that you were looking for a way to get rid of me tactfully."

"Was I?" He flicked a minute speck of something from the cuff of his jacket. "Well, you certainly gave me one, didn't you?"

"And how do you figure that?"

"You made a spectacle of yourself with the one man in the world whom you know I detest above all others and with very good reason. You let him ply you with champagne, then got into a car with him, aware not only of his driving record but of his sordid morals."

"For what it's worth, he behaved like a perfect gentleman."

"Then I can only say that your concept of the term differs vastly from mine, which shouldn't come as any great surprise to me, given your own atrocious behavior."

"Mine?" She stared at him, outraged.

"Yes, yours." Impassively, he stared back. "You arrived at the party with me, and in full view of people I've known all my life and who've treated you with exemplary courtesy and respect, you left with him. That might be acceptable in your circles, but it doesn't wash in mine. So add all that up, my dear Anne-Marie, and you'll understand, I'm sure, when I tell you that you can save your *I love you*'s for someone who wants to hear them, because I'm certainly not interested.''

''My goodness!'' she exclaimed. ''And to think I deluded myself for a second into thinking you might actually care about me!''

''I did care. I'm not in the habit of sleeping with a woman who isn't important to me.''

''But she'd better be perfect, just like you, or else she's history! No wonder your wife turned to another man. She probably couldn't stand living with a saint.''

White with anger, he lunged out of the chair. ''And you tempt me to forget I am a civilized man!''

''Well, that won't do, will it, Ethan? It might show you to be as full of human weakness as the next man.''

She'd gone too far. Much, much too far!

He advanced on her with such swift, lethal grace that she found herself inching toward the door. But his arm snaked out to trap her, and jerked her up against him. His mouth sealed itself against hers in a kiss so hard and explosive that she moaned in protest. Gradually, though, his lips softened in lingering seduction, and she turned fluid with weakness, and moaned for a different reason.

When the kiss ended, he caught her chin between his thumb and forefinger so that her face remained tilted up to his. ''You think I don't have my share of weaknesses? That I don't make mistakes and despise myself for them afterward?'' he asked in a low, savage voice. ''Then take a look at the self-loathing in my eyes right now, Anne-Marie, and think again!''

Then he tossed her aside as if she were no more than a piece of flotsam he'd found washed up on one of his precious, perfect beaches, and stalked out.

CHAPTER ELEVEN

THE wedding rehearsal took place the following evening. At nine in the morning, a servant delivered a note from Ethan, summoning Anne-Marie to the main house.

"What have you done to my nephew?" Josephine whispered, catching her in the inner courtyard, the second she arrived. "The temperature here drops to near-freezing every time he puts in an appearance! Should I take it the two of you have had a falling out?"

Before she could reply, Ethan showed up. "In here," he said, brusquely, jerking his thumb over his shoulder to a room at the east end of the lower hall.

Josephine gave Anne-Marie's arm a sympathetic squeeze. "I pray you emerge alive, child!"

The room was set up as an office. Leaving her to trail after him like the obedient subordinate he considered her to be, Ethan strode across the floor and sat down in a black leather chair behind a massive desk made of some exotic wood. "Have a seat," he said, in the same take-no-prisoners tone.

The only other chairs faced the window. With the sun still so low in the sky, the verandahs did little to diminish its glare.

Anne-Marie had not slept well. In fact, she hadn't slept at all. But she'd done a lot of useless crying, as her puffy eyes and blotchy complexion showed. She hardly needed to have it bathed in bright morning light, while the man responsible for all her misery looked as fresh and crisp as a newly-ironed shirt.

She hadn't weathered years of coping on her own without learning a thing or two, though. Betraying hurt feelings was a weakness which invited nothing but pity from the one who'd inflicted pain in the first place, so she remained just inside the door and said, "No thanks. And I don't know why you've sent for me, but it had better be important, because I've got a hundred other things waiting to be taken care of today."

"Then I'll get straight to the point," he said and, despite herself, she shivered, the lingering hope that perhaps he'd undergone a change of heart since she'd seen him last withering under the frost of his tone. Reaching into a drawer, he pulled out the outfit she'd made for Adrian and tossed it on the desk. It landed askew, like a rag doll flung aside by a petulant child. "We'll start with this."

"Am I to assume that you have a problem with it?"

"That you even need to ask tells me how little our tastes or expectations ever coincided."

She stepped forward and smoothed her hand over the finely-textured fabric. "And I suppose it doesn't matter to you one iota that Adrian chose this over a more conventional outfit, and is thrilled at the idea of wearing it?"

"Oh, he may wear it," Ethan said scornfully. "The next time he takes part in his school's annual play, that is, or at a friend's fancy-dress Christmas party. Under no circumstances, though, will he appear at a family wedding in it. But perhaps you forgot that's the reason you're here—or else you don't know the difference between the solemn rites of matrimony and a gaudy Hollywood extravaganza?"

"He's just a little boy, Ethan, and as ring bearer, he wanted to wear something distinctive and different."

"He will wear the morning suit created for him by my personal tailor."

"He'll be stuffed into something designed for a grown man, you mean? Good grief, you'll be expecting him to shave, next!"

"It's what I expect from you that you should be concerned about."

She sighed and rolled her eyes. "And now we get down to the real reason you hauled me up before your lordliness!"

Ignoring the barb, he said, "Our respective roles as maid of honor and best man mean we can't avoid one another until this wedding is over. But however much we might wish it were already done with, this time belongs to Solange and Philippe, and I will allow nothing to spoil it for them. Nor will I permit any behavior which might draw unfavorable attention to my family's name and reputation. Do we understand one another, Anne-Marie?"

"Perfectly," she snapped. "But just for the record, I'm agreeing to your terms solely out of respect for the other members of your family and for my best friend because, quite frankly, what you might want or not want no longer matters to me."

"Appearances are all that count," he said, swiveling the chair so that his back was toward her. "As long as we're in agreement on that, there's nothing more to be said. You may leave."

She'd have preferred to make a dignified exit, but his contempt sparked an anger in her which wouldn't go unsatisfied. "Who do you think you're talking to, you pompous jerk?" she spat, glaring at the back of his handsome, aristocratic head. "I'm not one of the underlings in your little puppet empire in which you, and only you, pull all the strings, and I will not take orders from you! Nor will I submit to becoming the chattel in your ridiculous turf war with Roberto Santos. I have done nothing—*nothing* to deserve being treated like this.''

"You have shown yourself to be untrustworthy and immature," he said flatly.

"While your conduct, of course, has been forever above reproach." Despite her best effort, her voice broke. "Somehow, no matter how hard I tried, where you were concerned, Ethan, it was never quite enough, was it? Your suspicions never quite faded away. Even when we were intimate together, you held something back. Not passion—that was beyond even your monumental self-control. You made love, but you didn't give love. You just lent it for a little while."

"What's the point in belaboring matters now, Anne-Marie?" he said stonily. "Nothing you say changes the fact that I thought you were different from the woman I married, but the first time the question of integrity arose, you showed yourself to be cut from the very same cloth."

"Did I really? Well, as a matter of interest, Ethan, would you have reacted quite as violently if I'd turned to any man other than Roberto Santos, last night?"

He swung back to face her, his features carved in stone. "As a matter of interest, would you have bothered to turn to any other man *but* Santos to advertise your displeasure with me? Wasn't that the whole point of your little exhibition?"

"No," she said, past caring about pride or dignity. "I was devastated by what I'd overheard, and he stepped in to save me from making a complete fool of myself in front of strangers. But if I'd had a choice, I'd rather it had been you who came to my rescue. Instead, you found a way to sneak ahead of me into my room, and ambushed me with recriminations before I had a chance to collect myself."

"Only a person with something to hide needs a chance to get her story straight."

"Something to hide?" she scoffed. "I'm not the one who smuggled a companion aboard my private jet and didn't say a word about it! But since we're having a tell-all session, just how did you manage to get back here before me, last night? And don't bother suggesting it was because I took my own sweet time, because Roberto drove me straight home."

"I took a shortcut through the jungle."

"In the dark? A likely tale!"

"You forget I was born on this island. I know its terrain as well as I know my own face."

"Then all I can say is that it's a pity you didn't cut through the impromptu conference with your Venezuelan friends with equal dispatch. We might not be having this conversation then."

"A man can't base his life on might-have-been's, Anne-Marie. He has to deal with what is. You and I come from different worlds. We were fools to believe we might find enough common ground to forge a lasting relationship, and the proof surely lies in the fact that a harmless incident was enough to sabotage our efforts."

"If you're talking about Desirée LaSalle," she said, drifting to the door so emotionally depleted that she felt hollow inside, "she's about as harmless as a black widow spider, and I hope for Adrian's sake that you realize it before she has you in her clutches."

"I can survive anything Desirée throws at me," he shot back. "After all, I survived Lisa. And you."

The rehearsal for the ceremony took place at five o'clock in the church in town, and as far as Anne-Marie was concerned, it might have been a foretaste of heaven for Solange and Philippe, but it was a prelude to hell for her.

Afterward, the bride's parents hosted a dinner party at the Plantation Club. It, too, was a ghastly experience made that much worse by the memory of the last time Anne-Marie had found herself there with Ethan.

Things between them had been so much more clear-cut when her chief impressions of him had been of sheer physical beauty overshadowed by stiff formality and overweening arrogance. But they'd been surface impressions only, revealing little of his capability for passion, and to be forced to sit so close to him now that she knew the difference caused her the most poignant agony.

How could she be expected to close her heart and mind to him when the faint scent of his soap tormented her with memories of the times they'd made love; of the taste and texture of his skin, the brush of his hand, the touch of his mouth? How was she supposed to equate all that with the cool, impassive man sitting beside her now, and not find herself awash in misery?

"I thought we had an agreement that we'd put aside our differences for now," he said, looking anywhere but at her, as the main course was cleared away.

"I'm trying."

"Then I suggest you try harder," he said unfeelingly. "You're not the only one who's suffered a setback, but you don't see me visibly wallowing in self-pity."

"I'm not you, Ethan. I don't have your steely ability to cut myself off from my emotions," she replied, staring into her wineglass and struggling to hang on to her self-control. She'd have succeeded, too, but the pitiful tremble in her voice gave her away.

"You might find it easier if you stopped swilling back

champagne,'' he informed her. ''At this rate, they're going to have to scrape you up off the floor before much longer.''

She turned to glare at him, outraged by the injustice of his accusation. ''I've hardly drunk anything but water!''

''I know,'' he said, with grim irony. ''But at least now you're annoyed enough to show a little life, instead of looking and acting like a corpse. 'Pale and interesting' does not become you.''

''I'm surprised you noticed!''

''Let's hope I'm the only one who does, because I meant what I said this morning. You've created enough trouble already, and I'll be damned if I'll stand by and let you cause more. *Nothing* is going to cast a cloud over my brother's wedding.''

''Stop trying to manage me, Ethan,'' she said waspishly. ''I won't be managed by you or anyone else.''

''You don't have any choice in the matter, my dear. The most you can do is take comfort in the fact that by tomorrow at this time, it'll all be over and you won't have to put up with me giving you orders ever again.''

''That's right.'' She dared to look him in the eye again and raised her glass in a mocking toast. ''Here's to going back to being the people we were before we met.''

But the truth was, she'd never be the same again. A broken woman had replaced the heart-whole, successful business entrepreneur who'd landed on Bellefleur well over a month ago and who was now gone for good. All those things she'd once thought important had been eclipsed by love for a man who didn't want her, and a little boy who needed her but couldn't have her.

That night, as always, he stopped by Adrian's room last thing. From the beginning, it had been his favorite time of day, with the house quiet around him and his son peacefully sleeping, but it had become particularly important since Lisa had left.

During those few quiet minutes, Ethan could search the child's face without worrying that his own might give away the doubts which hounded him. Could silently convey the words he wished he could speak openly.

Am I enough, mon petit? Do you blame me for your mother not being here? Should I have gone after her and brought her back, for your sake? Do you dream about her, miss her, cry for her when I'm not there to dry your tears? Do you worry that, one day, I, too, might leave and never come back?

Sometimes, a great upsurge of paternal love choked him and nothing would do but that he hold Adrian close, as he had when the boy was still an infant. Curbing the urge to hug him too fiercely, he'd cradle his son against his chest and attempt to absorb into his own cold soul the warm innocence and trust that childhood was all about.

Occasionally, the boy would stir, scour his eyes with a chubby fist, and murmur sleepily, "I love you, Papa," before falling instantly asleep again. At such times, Ethan's heart would swell with gratitude and he'd steal from the room, knowing he himself would sleep in peace.

Not tonight, though. Tonight, he felt more at a loss than he had the day his ex-wife had bailed out of motherhood and marriage, and he approached the bed with a heavy heart, dreading what he might find imprinted on his son's sleeping face.

The cheeks were flushed, the eyelashes a dark sweep of color, the mouth soft as a woman's. But the dried tear tracks told of the emotional storm which had taken place earlier, as did the foolish garment lying crumpled on the floor beside the bed.

Why can't I wear it? It's mine, and I like it!

It isn't suitable, my son.

But Anne-Marie made it specially for me. She said—

It doesn't matter what she said. She doesn't understand how we live on Bellefleur. She's not one of us.

She is so! Why do you always spoil everything? Anne-Marie will go away, the same as Mama did, and it's all your fault! I hate you, Papa!

About to reach out and smooth the unruly spill of hair on the pillow, Ethan stopped, afraid not that his touch might awaken his son, but that he himself wouldn't be able to bear the disillusionment he might find in those dark, sleepy eyes.

I brought this on both of us, he thought, sick with regret. *I have rocked the foundation of both our worlds by allowing her to grow close to us. If I'd paid attention to my instincts and kept her at a distance, things never would have come to this.*

A perfect sunrise greeted the wedding day. Awake early, Anne-Marie stepped out into a morning filled with birdsong and the scent of flowers.

I can do this, she told herself. *I can cope with everything I have to face today. I can walk down the aisle knowing Ethan's standing at the altar, and not let myself get swept away by impossible dreams. I won't pine for what I'm never going to have.*

She held on to that thought throughout the private breakfast with Solange, her parents, and the other bridesmaid, Angelique Tourneau. She managed to laugh when they went through the ritual of giving the bride "something old, something new, something borrowed, something blue." She swallowed hard when, an hour before the ceremony began, her hours of labor were rewarded by the sight of

Solange, blindingly radiant in her cloud of white silk organza, and told herself again, *I can do this! I can!*

When they gathered in the forecourt where two horse-drawn carriages waited to take them to the church, and she saw Adrian looking like a miniature of his father in the formal morning suit, she blinked and clamped her lips together and willed herself not to think about saying good-bye to him the next day. *One step at a time, Anne-Marie!* she ordered the quivering mass of emotion hidden under the pale aquamarine silk of her dress. *You can do this!*

"You look *so* beautiful, Anne-Marie," Adrian said, running up to clasp her hand and gazing up at her as if she were the most exquisite creature ever born. "Beautifuller than Solange. Beautifuller than anybody in the whole world!"

Just briefly, she almost broke down. Then, at the last second, she wrestled the huge lump in her throat into submission and sternly repeated her mantra. *I can do this!*

"And you're the most handsome young man I've ever seen," she managed, hoping he wouldn't notice how her voice wobbled and her smile kept slipping out of place.

Shortly after, with the faint echo of church bells drifting over the island, they climbed into the carriages and set off. Half the population of Bellefleur lined the sun-splashed roads, eager for a glimpse of bride as she passed by. The other half crowded the square in the center of town.

And throughout all that followed—entry into the old stone church, the processional up the aisle, and the ancient, beautiful words of the marriage ceremony—somehow, Anne-Marie held fast to her resolve. *I can do this!*

But, in the end, when it came time to take Ethan's arm and walk beside him in the recessional march back down the aisle, she could not do it, after all. The sheer willpower which had carried her that far evaporated, and she started to shake so badly that her little bouquet of gardenias trembled as if caught in a sudden breeze.

"Hold on," Ethan murmured, his free hand reaching over to steady her. "It's almost over."

It wasn't, though. She had to pose beside him for interminable photographs. Had to join him in the carriage on the return journey to the villa. Had to sit beside him during the long, elaborate reception, and smile graciously when he toasted her and thanked her for all she'd done to make the day so memorable. Then, as the early tropical twilight descended and a thousand candles added to the moonlight spilling through the lacy iron doors of the inner courtyard, she had to dance with him. Feel his arm around her, his thigh brushing against hers, his hand warm and compelling in the small of her back.

It was too much. Too painful, too ironic, too everything!

"I can't take much more of this," she said, squeezing her eyes shut against the persistent prick of tears.

"Of me, you mean?"

"Of us."

"There is no 'us.' There never was, not really. The way I see it, having you step in as my hostess lulled us both into a false sense that we belonged together, that we were a couple, and we somehow forgot it was all just pretense."

"Blame everything on that, if you like, but what really sank us is that you lied to me by omission and didn't like being caught at it."

"By all means believe that, if it makes you feel better," he said. "The important thing is that we came to our senses before any lasting damage was done."

Oh, how she envied him his resilience! And how, for a brief, blessed moment, she hated him for emerging unscathed when she herself was wounded to the core. "Speak for yourself, Ethan, but don't ever presume to know what

I'm feeling! *You're* the one who sabotaged our relationship, and I've had about enough of listening to you trying to rationalize your way out of it.''

He swung her into one last turn as the music died, and released her. ''Then you'll be relieved to know the ordeal's almost over,'' he said. ''It looks as if the newlyweds are preparing to leave. Better join the other unmarried hopefuls milling around the bride.''

''No,'' she said, a terrible chill chasing over her where, a moment before, she'd felt the warmth of his touch.

''Yes,'' he said, taking her elbow and almost dragging her toward the grand staircase where Solange stood four steps up, ready to toss her bouquet over her shoulder. ''It's expected of you.''

She shrugged herself free of his grip. ''Fine! I'll perform this one last service, and then I'll be free of you and all your inflexible, impossible *expectations!*''

Disgruntled, disheartened, she deliberately stood apart from the women clustered eagerly at the foot of the stairs. Let one of them catch the damned flowers, if being the next bride meant so much to them! After her recent experience with love, marriage came so far down her list of priorities that it didn't rate a mention.

But either Solange had lousy aim, or the demons weren't yet done tormenting Anne-Marie, because the bouquet sailed clean over all those immaculately coiffed heads and aimed directly for her. Instinctively, she reached up and caught it—it was either that, or have it smack her squarely in the face.

It appeared to be a popular decision. Everyone cheered and applauded. Everyone, that was, but Ethan because, when she turned to acknowledge the crowd, he was no longer part of it.

CHAPTER TWELVE

She was packed and ready to leave by ten the next day. The letter to Ethan was written, she'd phoned Morton to arrange for her luggage to be brought up to the main house and for a car to take her to the airport. All that remained was to pay one last visit to Josephine. At that hour, she'd be taking coffee on the verandah outside the morning salon.

Curiously numb, Anne-Marie stopped to take one last look around the guest pavilion. Already it wore the deserted air of a place filled only with ghosts, but they'd be chased away soon enough, when the next batch of visitors arrived. Would that she could be as easily rid of them!

Burying a sigh, she turned and walked slowly through the gardens, memory after memory layering her mind. Here was the trail where she'd ridden behind him on horseback, her body still sweetly singing from their lovemaking, and here the koi pond where she'd first seen him. And finally, as she emerged from the shade of the overhanging greenery, and followed the winding path to the south terrace, there the big infinity pool where he'd forced her into an impromptu swimming lesson.

As expected, Josephine sat in her usual high-backed wicker chair, a tray on the table before her. "What do you mean, you're leaving?" she demanded, pausing in the middle of refilling her coffee cup, and regarding Anne-Marie with a mixture of surprise and indignation. "Child, I expected you'd stay at least another week. Now that all the excitement's over and we have the place to ourselves again, I was looking forward to our spending some quiet time together.''

"I'm sorry to disappoint you, but I simply can't do that, Madame Duclos. I don't belong here, and now that Solange and Philippe have left for their honeymoon, there's no reason for me to stay. But I couldn't leave without first telling you how much your friendship has come to mean to me.''

"Friendship? Child, you're part of my family, and blood ties be damned!''

Family. The one thing she missed so much. Oh, if only it were possible to be absorbed into this one! But it couldn't be. She had no interest in becoming Ethan's adopted sister or cousin.

"That's the nicest thing you could have said to me,'' she sniffled, forgetting any idea she'd entertained that she might make a dignified exit, "and I love you for it, I really do.''

"Enough to start calling this old woman *Tante* Josephine, and keep her company a while longer?''

"I'd be honored to call you Aunt, but....'' She fought a losing battle with the lump in her throat and choked out, "I have to go.''

"Things didn't work out with Ethan, then?'' Josephine eyed her shrewdly. "I suspected as much, the way you both behaved yesterday.''

"Were we very obvious?''

"Only to me, child. Suffice it to say, I'm very sorry.''

"The odds were against us from the beginning.''

"Isn't it possible, if you stayed, that the two of you might be able to work things out?''

"No.'' A single tear tracked down her face. Wiping it away, Anne-Marie looked out at the hummingbirds fighting over territorial rights in the garden. Such beautiful creatures, but so fiercely protective of their own! Had they taken lessons from Ethan, she wondered. "You yourself warned me, the second night I was here, that once Ethan makes up his mind, nothing changes it. And I'm afraid he's made up his mind about me."

Josephine sighed and laid her head against the back of her chair. "It would appear that you've made up yours, too."

"Yes."

"You'll be coming back you know. Often. We won't have it any other way."

"Perhaps I will. But not for a long time."

"Because of my nephew?"

"Because I'm not very good at saying goodbye. Which is why I'm going to ask you to give this to Ethan for me." She dropped the letter on the table. "I really can't face seeing him again."

"You don't have to," Josephine said wearily. "He left for Venezuela last night, immediately after the wedding was over." She hauled herself upright and fixed Anne-Marie in one of her penetrating stares. "If you're adamant about leaving, I'll do as you ask and give him your note when he returns, but I will *not* act as your messenger with Adrian. He'll be devastated if you leave without seeing him."

"I know." Anne-Marie swallowed. "I dread having to tell him. I've come to love him—to love *all* of you, dearly."

"As we have come to love you, *ma chère*—those of us with any sense, at least." She eased herself out of the chair and held out her arms. "Give me a hug to remember you by until we meet again."

Half-blind with tears, Anne-Marie went to her, kissed

her cheek and inhaled the delicate, powdery fragrance that was Josephine.

I'll never smell heliotrope again without thinking of her, she thought, as another tear slipped loose. *"Au revoir, ma tante."*

A discreet cough from within the morning salon ended the moment. "The car is waiting to take you to the airport whenever you're ready, *Mademoiselle,*" Morton announced. "And I have advised the pilot that you'll be needing the jet to take you to the mainland."

Voice cracking, Josephine murmured, *"Au revoir,* child, and Godspeed."

Not trusting herself to speak again, Anne-Marie nodded, pressed a last kiss to her cheek, and followed the butler out to the forecourt. There, Adrian huddled in the shade of a coconut palm, his little face creased with misery.

"I don't want you to go," he whimpered, the minute he saw her. "Please, *please,* don't!"

She hadn't thought she had the capacity to endure any more angst, but the sight and sound of him dealt yet another blow to her battered heart. "Oh, Adrian, I'd stay if I could."

"That's what everybody always says," he cried, "but they go anyway and leave me by myself. First Maman left, then Papa went away, and now you're going."

"But Papa will be home again soon," she said, kneeling in front of him and gathering him close. "He always comes back, darling, you know that."

Adrian, though, had worked himself up into such a state that he was inconsolable. "No," he sobbed against her neck. "He went away because I was bad. He doesn't like me anymore."

"You're never bad," she said, shocked that he'd even

think such a thing. "You're the best little boy in the whole world, and your papa adores you."

"Not anymore," he said again, a fresh spate of tears shaking his little body. "Nobody likes me anymore. They don't even notice I'm here."

Anne-Marie raised her eyes, mutely asking for help in coping with the situation from the nanny hovering in the background. The nanny stared back, unable to offer any. And in all fairness, how could she be expected to, when much of what Adrian said was true?

Apart from his brief role in yesterday's ceremony, he'd been shunted aside in all the pre-wedding hype of the last few days. And now that it was over, the people he most relied on were abandoning him, one by one, first with Solange leaving, then Ethan, and now she herself.

"I'm so sorry," she murmured, kissing his mop of soft, dark hair. "I'd stay if I could, but if I don't leave now, I'll miss my flight."

"No, you won't," he wept, lifting his tear-drenched face to hers. "It's Papa's jet, and it won't go 'til you tell it to. You *don't* have to go yet, Anne-Marie. You could stay a little bit longer if you really wanted to…if you really loved me the way I love you!"

If she hadn't come to know him well enough to recognize that he was the least likely child in the world to resort without cause to such a torrent of emotional blackmail, she wouldn't have caved in. But even a stranger could have seen his distress was genuine, and she couldn't turn away from him. Her bruised heart wouldn't allow it; it had taken enough punishment.

"I suppose I could stay another day or two," she conceded, "but only until Papa comes home. You do understand that, Adrian, don't you?"

His lip quivered. "Yes."

She looked over to where the ever-patient Morton waited at the car, and shrugged. "You must have heard."

He inclined his head. *"Oui, mademoiselle."*

"I'm sorry for the inconvenience—"

"Not at all," he said sympathetically. *"Monsieur's* son is more important. We all understand."

Josephine's response was much less restrained when she learned of the change in plans. "Well, hallelujah!" she exclaimed, her wise old eyes suddenly misting over. "Adrian succeeded where I failed, and managed to talk some sense into you!"

"It's only until Ethan comes back," Anne-Marie cautioned her. "Please let's all be clear on that."

"We'll take whatever we can get. *Mademoiselle* will be staying here in the main house, Morton. Put her bags in the suite beside Adrian's. The boy will feel better knowing she's close by, and so will I."

Surprisingly, so did Anne-Marie, for all that she'd been so anxious to leave before. Without the fear that Ethan might show up at any minute, the slow and easy pace of island life soothed her troubled soul, and the day drifted past, its tranquility broken only by quiet conversation, the clink of china during lunch and afternoon tea, and the sound of Adrian's laughter as he splashed in the pool.

That evening, she kept him company while he ate a light supper, then tucked him into bed, read him a story, and at his request, listened while he said his prayers.

"Make Anne-Marie stay forever, heavenly father," he ordered, closing his eyes and clasping his hands, "and that's all for today because I'm tired."

Clearly, he had a unique relationship with God!

Hiding a smile, Anne-Marie tiptoed out of the room and joined Louis and Josephine for dinner on the terrace. It was dark by then, and although the sky overhead remained clear, the usual late onshore breeze had died, leaving the atmosphere thick and breathless. By the time the meal was over, a line of cloud creeping up from the south had obscured the stars.

"We're in for a spell of bad weather," Louis remarked, leading the way inside. "Hurricane season's come early this year."

They were lingering over coffee and cognac when the tranquility came to an abrupt end—not, as might have been expected, because of the approaching storm, but by the arrival of the chief of Bellefleur's tiny police force.

"Forgive me for interrupting your evening, but I've received a report from the authorities in Caracas," he began, and his tone alone was enough to tell them he wasn't bringing good news. "*Monsieur* Beaumont left there by helicopter this morning, en route to an oil platform some seventy miles from the Venezuelan coast. However, possibly because of adverse conditions, he never arrived at his destination, nor has he been heard from since."

Josephine turned as pale as parchment and reached for Louis's hand. "Have they sent out a search party?"

"*Non, madame.* By the time anyone knew he was missing, night had fallen, but they will start looking at first light tomorrow."

"Who else was with him?" Louis asked shakily.

"No one."

"*No one?*" Anne-Marie smothered a gasp. "He flew out there alone, knowing the weather was poor?"

"*Oui, Mademoiselle,* but he is an experienced pilot." The chief backed toward the door, his expression grave. "I'm very sorry to be the bearer of such distressing news. Be assured every effort will be made to bring *Monsieur* Beaumont home safely again."

"You'll keep us informed?" Louis said.

"Of course, *monsieur*. As soon as I hear anything, I will be in touch. I am certain we will receive good news in the morning."

But they didn't, not that day, or the next, or the one after that. Instead, the weather responsible for his disappearance closed in over the island in a series of storms which left the garden littered with debris.

Not once during that time did Anne-Marie cry, because to do so would have been to admit the worst—that Ethan would never come home again. And that she couldn't bear to dwell on. A world without Ethan simply wasn't a world she wanted to be part of.

"We have to have faith," she told an increasingly distraught Josephine. "We have to believe he's coming back, for all our sakes, especially Adrian's. He needs his father."

But with the staff aware and talking among themselves of the disaster which had struck, eventually there was no keeping the news from the child. He couldn't be allowed to find out by accident that his beloved papa was missing.

No one expected he'd take the news well, but nor was anyone prepared for the way he responded. "It's my fault," he said, in a bleak, resigned little voice, when they explained that there'd been a storm at sea. "I wished bad things and now they've happened. I told Papa I hated him, and now he's dead."

"No, darling," they rushed to assure him. "Papa is just lost, and it was an accident. Nobody's to blame. Certainly not you."

But there was no moving him. "It was me. I did it," he said, and when they tried to hold him and comfort him, he wriggled free and ran up to his room.

"Let him be, child," Josephine said sadly, when Anne-Marie made to go after him. "He's his father's son, taking the blame for everything that goes wrong, and shutting himself off from those who love him, to bleed in private. That's just their way. He'll come to us when he's ready, you'll see.''

But when noon arrived and still Adrian hadn't reappeared, Anne-Marie couldn't bear it a moment longer. It wasn't natural for a child so young to be bear such a crushing burden of unfounded guilt alone. It wasn't right.

''I've come to take Adrian down to lunch,'' she told the maid she found changing the bed linen in his room.

''He's not here,'' the girl replied.

''Do you know where he went?''

''*Non, mademoiselle.* He said only that he was going to find his papa.''

A chill ran over Anne-Marie. There'd been no sign of the child for over an hour. If he'd come downstairs, it had been stealthily enough for none of them to notice.

Unwilling to heap further stress on the frail shoulders of the old couple waiting so anxiously for word of their missing nephew, she told the girl, ''We have to find that child. Help me search the rooms up here.''

But although they scoured every inch of the upper floor, and roped in other staff members to look in every nook and cranny of the main floor, all they found was Adrian's kitten curled up asleep under a chair. Of Adrian himself, there wasn't a sign.

''And why would he be here?'' Anne-Marie exclaimed, running a despairing hand through her hair. ''If he was going to look for his father, it makes sense that he'd go outside. We're looking in the wrong place!''

''But he knows that his father wasn't on the island when he became lost,'' Morton reminded her. ''He won't find him in the garden and it's not possible for him to open the main gates and escape onto the road, so he must still be here somewhere.''

A logical enough assumption, but Anne-Marie's relief was short-lived as another possibility occurred to her, one so terrifying that she couldn't bring herself to utter it aloud.

Instead, she said, "Please go about your normal business and don't say a word to alarm *Monsieur* or *Madame* Duclos. Serve lunch as usual, and if they ask where I am, tell them I've gone for a stroll and will be back shortly."

"A stroll? In this weather?" Morton raised skeptical eyebrows. "*Mademoiselle,* I doubt they will accept such an explanation."

"I'm used to wind and rain," she told him. "And that's the reason you give them, should they question you. But under no circumstance do you let them know that Adrian is missing and I've gone looking for him."

"Forgive me, *Mademoiselle,* but it is more than my job here is worth for me to let you put yourself at risk. I must insist on knowing what you plan to do."

"I think that boy's gone down to the beach," she said, looking the man straight in the eye and not even blinking at telling only half the truth. "He knows his father was lost at sea. In his mind, he expects that's how he'll come home again, and he's down there waiting for him."

Please let that be all he's done! she prayed, racing through the gardens, not to the steps below the guest pavilion, but to that other trail which led to a different part of the beach, and to the boathouse.

In places, the way was slippery and so thick with mud that it sucked at her feet, impeding her progress even though the hillside sloped in her favor. The return journey would be uphill all the way. If she'd guessed wrong and Adrian wasn't at the beach, it would take her another half hour to make it back to the house and raise the general alarm.

Half an hour—half a minute!—lost in the search for a

missing child could mean the difference between life and death.

But intuition was stronger than fear. He'd come this way, she was certain. And as she skidded around the last corner to where the trees thinned out and the shore came into view, she saw a sodden red running shoe, which she recognized as Adrian's, lying in the middle of the path, and knew she'd been right to follow her instincts.

Clutching at the overhanging vines to keep her balance, she fought her way over the remaining distance and, breathless from the exertion, jumped down to the sand. To her left, the boathouse rose up, its wide door standing open, its interior empty. And at the sight, everything in her hung in fearful suspension—her breathing, her heart, and the hope which had driven her this far.

With slow dread, she turned her head and looked to the right. The normally placid blue sea heaved and rolled restlessly in choppy green waves across the narrow bay. Beyond the shelter of the headland, whitecaps dotted the horizon. And some fifty yards from shore, a small boy in a red life jacket clung to the tiller of a sailboat being tossed around like a matchbox.

Until that moment, she hadn't thought matters could get any worse, that she could be more terrified or had more to lose than was already lost. Yet even as she stood there, paralyzed with horror, the boat yawed erratically, and the wind whipped the sail to one side, then slammed it back to the other with enough force to flatten the dingy so completely that the hull lifted clear out of the water.

And when the boat righted itself again, there was no longer a little boy wearing a red life jacket clinging to the tiller. There was nothing but the sail flapping limply as the vessel turned its nose into the wind.

"Adrian!" she screamed, searching the churning waters until her eyes burned.

But the wind took his name, tore it to shreds, and flung it away.

CHAPTER THIRTEEN

THEY didn't hear him come in and he stood for a moment on the threshold, watching them. They sat close together, she with her head on his shoulder, and he with his arm around her. They'd been like that for as long as he could remember: a couple who allowed nothing to come between them, not even the grief so evident in their posture now.

A pang of regret shot through him that he should be the cause of their unhappiness, when they'd brought to his life nothing but unlimited joy and affection. "I heard a rumor that I was dead," he said, stepping fully into the room. "I hope you haven't planned an elaborate funeral. I'd hate to see it go to waste."

They sprang up from the sofa as if they were closer to thirty than seventy, and it was almost worth what he'd gone through over the last three days, just to see the way their faces lit up, and the spring in their step as they came toward him.

"I don't believe in wasting good money on funerals," his aunt said. "I planned a wake instead, and invited everyone on the island."

But Louis didn't have her stamina or resilience, and broke into choking sobs when he tried to speak.

"Now see what you've done, you fool!" she scolded Ethan. "It's a miracle you didn't give him a heart attack!"

None too sure he had as firm a grip on his own emotions as he'd have liked, he wrapped his arms around both of them. "I'm sorry I worried you. If I could have prevented

176

it, I would have. But it's over. I'm here and as you can see, all in one piece.''

"Yes," Josephine said severely. "And you have some explaining to do. Start at the beginning and don't leave out a thing."

"I will," he said, laughing for what seemed like the first time in years. "But first I need a stiff drink. I think we all do. Morton!"

The butler came at a run, his face mirroring the same stunned amazement Josephine and Louis had shown shortly before. "Good heavens!" he exclaimed, turning a little gray around the edges.

"Relax, Morton," Ethan said. "I'm not a ghost, just a very weary man who could use a single malt Scotch, straight up. And pour one for yourself, while you're at it. You look as if you could use it."

"Scotch?" Josephine scoffed. "This calls for champagne. Don't look so woebegone, Morton! The nightmare's over."

"I'm afraid not," the butler said, and Ethan didn't like the man's shifty-eyed expression one little bit.

"What is it? What aren't you telling us?" he said sharply, the utter and unusual silence throughout the rest of the house suddenly dawning on him. "And where's my son?"

"He's in his room," Josephine said. "We kept quiet as long as we could, Ethan, but when no news of your whereabouts had come after three days, we felt we had to tell him you'd gone missing. But he'll be so happy to see his papa again. Get someone to bring him down, will you, Morton?"

The butler shuffled uneasily from one foot to the other. "I'm afraid I can't, *madame*. Young Adrian's gone missing too, you see. We've looked everywhere in the house, and he's not to be found."

Refusing to give in to the thread of panic uncurling in the pit of his stomach, Ethan said, "Well, he can't have gone far. We'll search the grounds."

"*Mademoiselle* Barclay has gone already to do that. She believes the boy might have wandered to the beach to look for you, *monsieur*."

"How long ago did she leave?" Ethan barked, his satisfaction at hearing Anne-Marie hadn't yet left for Canada marred by the news that his son was missing.

"Nearly half an hour, *monsieur*."

"And you've waited until now to mention it? Good God, man, what were you thinking?"

"She asked me not to say anything until she returned," Morton said miserably. "She didn't want to upset *Madame* Josephine or *Monsieur* Louis unnecessarily."

"Alert the outdoor staff," Ethan said, heading for the terrace at a run. "Have them cover the entire estate, including all accessible sections of shoreline. And get a search team out on the water."

She was out of her depth. The waves slapped at her face, stole her breath, threatened to overwhelm her. But at least the wind had lessened some, and she was closing in on the boat.

Adrian couldn't drown. He was wearing a life jacket. The water was warm, the tide running toward shore.

She lifted her head, searching...searching. Tried again to call his name. And was slapped again by another wave.

The salt water rushed into her mouth and up her nose. Choking, panic-stricken, she flailed her arms, and made contact with something—the hard, shiny shell of the dingy's hull. Then another wave rolled over her, and the boat slipped away.

I can't do this, she thought, but knew she couldn't give up until she found him, or drowned trying. She owed it to the child and to everyone who loved him. But her arms were leaden weights, her legs aching, and her lungs burning.

The boat heaved up in front of her again, and with the last of her strength she lunged for it. And missed.

It bobbed away, as buoyant as she was inept. Then, catching another wave, it floated toward her again, and this time ran over her.

Eyes wide open with terror, she went under, and bowed to the might of the sea. Green and merciless, it tumbled around her.

This was the end, and that was just as well. She could never have faced the Beaumonts again, knowing that she hadn't been able to save Adrian.

But drowning, so she'd heard, was supposed to be painless, once a person gave up the struggle. So why was her scalp hurting, and what was the dark shape looming above her? A shark? *Oh, please let me die before it attacks!* was her last coherent thought.

The tension on her hair increased, yanking her up hard toward the light. Then, like a cork popping out of a champagne bottle and with her lungs fit to burst, she resurfaced and found herself looking straight into the only patches of blue left on earth. Ethan's enraged eyes.

"How many times do I have to do this, before you learn?" he shouted over the clamor of the waves.

Oh, yes, she was dead. Even worse, she'd been sent to hell!

Warily, she opened her eyes a fraction. A late afternoon sun had broken through the leaden skies and played over the cool, cotton sheets covering her. *Hell*, she thought blearily, *looked very much like her room in the Beaumont villa*.

And the devil sounded just like Ethan! "So you're awake finally," he said, and turning her head, she found him slouched in a chair next to the bed.

She ached all over and her throat felt as if it had been put through a meat grinder. "I didn't know I'd been asleep," she croaked, struggling to reconstruct the events which had led up to the present moment.

Something dreadful had happened. She'd been afraid. Exhausted. Stricken with unbearable grief.

Then she remembered, and a great wash of misery flowed over her. "Ah, no!" she moaned, covering her face as the tears spurted from her eyes. "Adrian...!"

"Adrian's in better shape than you, you'll be happy to hear. But then, he showed a lot more sense."

It took a moment for her to absorb what he was telling her. At length, she lowered her hands and dared to look at him again. "Adrian's...*alive?*"

"He's alive."

She shook her head, wanting to believe, but afraid to. "How is that possible? There was no sign—"

"That's a very seaworthy little boat."

"And he's a very little boy!"

"But smart," Ethan said. "I'd taught him always to wear a safety line, and he knew enough to brace himself low in the cockpit, and wait to be rescued or washed ashore."

She digested that for a space. "What if he'd been carried out to sea?"

"He knew he wouldn't be. The currents in the bay sweep toward the beach. Why else do you think it's so littered with shells and driftwood?'' His voice softened fractionally. ''Relax, Anne-Marie. He really is perfectly fine.''

''And you?'' She half sat up and tentatively touched his arm. It felt reassuringly solid and warm. Still, she had to ask. ''Are you fine, too?''

''Afraid so.''

She let out a long, heartfelt sigh and flopped back against the pillows. ''Oh, thank God!'' she said hoarsely and with profound reverence. *''Thank God!''*

''Here,'' Ethan said, pouring liquid over ice cubes in a glass. ''Drink some of this. It's lemonade. It'll soothe your throat.''

She took a few sips, then glanced at him again. ''You wouldn't lie to me, Ethan, would you? Adrian really is safe?''

''Do you think I'd be sitting here with you, if he wasn't? Yes, he's safe. He's downstairs with my aunt and uncle, stuffing himself with cream cakes. If you're up to it, though, he'd probably like to pay you a visit.''

''Oh, yes,'' she said. ''Please!''

He picked up the house phone and punched in a number. ''She's awake and ready to receive company,'' he said.

He'd barely had time to hang up before the door opened to admit Adrian, Josephine and Louis. Only then, when she could see with her own eyes that things were just as Ethan had said, did Anne-Marie truly believe him.

''Well,'' Josephine said to him, when the excitement had simmered down some. ''Did you ask her?''

''Not yet,'' he replied.

''Ask me what?'' Anne-Marie said.

''Nothing that can't wait,'' he said, and lifted Adrian onto the bed.

''Tell her how you escaped, Papa,'' Adrian begged.

"Tell her how your radio didn't work and how you had to land on a deserted island and eat raw fish for three whole days."

Ethan looked at her, and she went hot all over. Whatever else had changed in the last few days, his effect on her was still the same. "He thinks I'm the reincarnation of Robinson Crusoe," he said. "Actually, I had enough supplies on board to last me a week."

"Is that why you took your sweet time coming home?" she said, basking in the warmth of his smile.

"No," he said. "Even if I hadn't managed to damage the helicopter when I brought it down, the weather didn't let up enough for me to leave."

"So how did you get away again?"

"I finally figured out how to fix the radio, and called for help."

"And they came and got him," Adrian said gleefully, bouncing on the mattress. "Now, tell her how you rescued me, Papa!"

"We'll talk about that some other time," Josephine intervened, her sharp gaze missing nothing. "I think Anne-Marie's had all the excitement she can take for now. Come along, Adrian. Let's leave her to get some rest."

"You should go with them," Anne-Marie said, when Ethan made no move to follow them. "Adrian was devastated when he heard you'd gone missing. I imagine it's going to take him a while to get over being afraid."

He paid not the slightest attention. "And what about you, Anne-Marie?" he said instead. "Were you so devastated that you turned to Roberto Santos for comfort?"

"Oh, I was pretty devastated at the time," she admitted, all her nice, warm fuzzy feeling evaporating. "But you're being so horrible now that I have to wonder why I even cared."

"I find myself wondering why you weren't already headed back to Vancouver when the news came through that I'd turned up missing."

"I stayed here to be with your son. He really needed you, of course, but you decided business was more important."

"I don't need you to tell me how to be a father."

"Well, someone has to!"

"And you think you're qualified to do that, do you? You, who've never had a child?"

"I might never have given birth, but this much I do know. You might be a prince in the eyes of your lowly island subjects, Ethan Beaumont, but to me you're just an arrogant, uncaring jerk who takes pleasure in trampling all over other people's feelings, and I hate you!"

"Oh, good," he purred, joining her on the bed and sweeping her into his arms. "You really are going to make a full recovery, *mon amour*. You had me worried there, for a while."

And then he kissed her. It was a very long, very satisfying kiss.

"I beg your pardon?" she said, when at last he lifted his mouth from hers and she got back her breath. "What did you call me?"

"You heard." He played with her fingers and she realized with astonishment that he was having a very hard time keeping his voice steady. "I called you 'my love.'"

"Oh," she said. Then, nervously, "Am I hallucinating?"

He cleared his throat. "*Non, ma très chère Anne-Marie.* It is a testament to my stupid male pride, I suppose, that only when I found myself staring death in the face did I realize how badly I wanted to live long enough to tell you that I love you. All the time I wrestled with that infernal radio, I thought of you. Remembered the smell of your hair, your skin—almond cream with a hint of tangerine. It's what gave me the strength to persevere.''

"But how much do you love me?" she said.

He kissed her again. "More than you can begin to imagine," he said against her lips.

"Enough to marry me?"

He drew back, his blue eyes wide with shock. "Aren't you jumping the gun a little?"

"No," she said. "Because I love you, too, and I love Adrian. A lot. I didn't know it was possible to feel like this—to be so full of wanting to give everything—*everything,* Ethan!—just to make someone else happy. But if that's more than you can accept, then you might love me, but you don't love me enough."

He regarded her solemnly for a long, thoughtful minute. "You stayed when you could have walked away," he said at last. "You welcomed me into your arms, your bed, your heart. You continue to be the best thing that ever happened to me. How could I not love you enough? But when it comes to marriage—"

"It's out of the question because I'm not an island woman and you're afraid I'll turn out to be just like your ex-wife." She turned away, her hopes falling around her like ashes.

He caught her hands and forced her to look at him again. "No," he said. "Not that, at all. What I was going to say is that before you decide you want to be my wife, you need to recognize the baggage I bring with me. Not just Adrian—"

"Adrian is your son, Ethan. That alone is reason enough for me to love him."

"He's also another woman's child. Can you live with the fact that, if she were to come back and want to be part of his life, much though I'd hate it, I'd have to allow it because I don't have the right to deny him his mother?''

"Can you live with the fact that, if she doesn't, I might never be able to fill her empty shoes? That Adrian will always know I'm not his birth mother?''

"It's not your job to try to replace Lisa, my love, because you're nothing like her. You're you—and you're perfect just as you are.''

"Nobody's perfect, Ethan,'' she said, ''and it's dangerous to believe otherwise. You just leave yourself open to disappointment.''

"Then let me amend the statement and say that you're perfect for me. You're beautiful, and stubborn, and smart, and unafraid to stand your ground. You're what I need. You temper my arrogance and remind me I'm as flawed as the next man. You keep me grounded. But then I look at it from your point of view, and see only the sacrifices you'd be making if you married me.''

"Well, of course I would,'' she said. ''And so would you. Loving someone doesn't come cheap. It demands sacrifice and compromise. It means caring about the other person's needs more than caring about your own.'' She stopped and drew in a painful breath. ''And that's how much I love you, Ethan. Enough to let you go, if that's what you need.''

"The hell you will!'' he said softly, stroking her face. "I have no intention of letting you go. Ever.''

A knock came at the door and Josephine popped her head into the room. ''Forgive me for interrupting, Ethan, but we can't wait a minute longer to find out. Have you proposed to her yet?''

"No,'' he said, pressing a kiss to Anne-Marie's hair. "She asked me first. And I accepted.''

"Excellent!" Josephine said. "I'll tell Morton to break out the champagne. Shall we have it served in the salon?"

"By all means," Ethan said, "but don't expect us to join you for a while. We have other business to conduct first and if it's all the same to you, *ma tante,* I'd like to do it in private."

"Of course. Take all the time you need," she said, and left them alone.

"I need a lifetime," Ethan said, his gaze scorching over Anne-Marie. "But I've learned in the last few days that we're guaranteed nothing except this moment. Let's make it one that lasts as long as we have the breath and strength to say 'I love you.' Let's make it last forever, my lovely Anne-Marie."

"Oui, mon amour," she said, touching his mouth with her fingertip. "Let's do that."

And then they stopped talking, and got down to the other business.

The world's bestselling romance series.

HARLEQUIN®
Presents~

Seduction and Passion Guaranteed!

RED HOT REVENGE

There are times in a man's life...
when only seduction will setttle old scores!

Pick up our exciting new series of revenge-filled romances—
they're recommended and red-hot!

Coming soon:

MISTRESS ON LOAN by Sara Craven
On sale August, #2338

THE MARRIAGE DEBT by Daphne Clair
On sale September, #2347

Available wherever Harlequin books are sold.

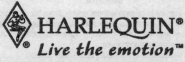

HARLEQUIN®
® *Live the emotion*™

Visit us at www.eHarlequin.com

HPRHR

If you enjoyed what you just read,
then we've got an offer you can't resist!

Take 2 bestselling
love stories FREE!
Plus get a FREE surprise gift!

Clip this page and mail it to Harlequin Reader Service®

IN U.S.A.	IN CANADA
3010 Walden Ave.	P.O. Box 609
P.O. Box 1867	Fort Erie, Ontario
Buffalo, N.Y. 14240-1867	L2A 5X3

YES! Please send me 2 free Harlequin Presents® novels and my free surprise gift. After receiving them, if I don't wish to receive anymore, I can return the shipping statement marked cancel. If I don't cancel, I will receive 6 brand-new novels every month, before they're available in stores! In the U.S.A., bill me at the bargain price of $3.57 plus 25¢ shipping & handling per book and applicable sales tax, if any*. In Canada, bill me at the bargain price of $4.24 plus 25¢ shipping & handling per book and applicable taxes**. That's the complete price and a savings of at least 10% off the cover prices—what a great deal! I understand that accepting the 2 free books and gift places me under no obligation ever to buy any books. I can always return a shipment and cancel at any time. Even if I never buy another book from Harlequin, the 2 free books and gift are mine to keep forever.

106 HDN DNTZ
306 HDN DNT2

Name _____ (PLEASE PRINT)

Address _____ Apt.# _____

City _____ State/Prov. _____ Zip/Postal Code _____

* Terms and prices subject to change without notice. Sales tax applicable in N.Y.
** Canadian residents will be charged applicable provincial taxes and GST.
All orders subject to approval. Offer limited to one per household and not valid to current Harlequin Presents® subscribers.
® are registered trademarks of Harlequin Enterprises Limited.

PRES02   ©2001 Harlequin Enterprises Limited

eHARLEQUIN.com

Becoming an eHarlequin.com member is easy,
fun and **FREE!** Join today to enjoy great benefits:

- **Super savings** on all our books, including
  members-only discounts and offers!

- Enjoy **exclusive online reads**—FREE!

- Info, tips and **expert advice** on writing
  your own romance novel.

- FREE romance **newsletters,**
  customized by you!

- Find out the latest on your
  favorite authors.

- Enter to win exciting **contests
  and promotions!**

- Chat with other members in our
  community message boards!

**Plus, we'll send you 2 FREE Internet-exclusive
eHarlequin.com books (no strings!)
just to say thanks for joining us online.**

**To become a member,
visit www.eHarlequin.com today!**

INTMEMB

Is your man too good to be true?

Hot, gorgeous AND romantic?
If so, he could be a Harlequin® Blaze™ series cover model!

Our grand-prize winners will receive a trip for two to New York City to shoot the cover of a Blaze novel, and will stay at the luxurious Plaza Hotel.

Plus, they'll receive $500 U.S. spending money!

The runner-up winners will receive $200 U.S. to spend on a romantic dinner for two.

It's easy to enter!

In 100 words or less, tell us what makes your boyfriend or spouse a true romantic and the perfect candidate for the cover of a Blaze novel, and include in your submission two photos of this potential cover model.

All entries must include the written submission of the contest entrant, two photographs of the model candidate and the Official Entry Form and Publicity Release forms completed in full and signed by both the model candidate and the contest entrant. Harlequin, along with the experts at Elite Model Management, will select a winner.

For photo and complete Contest details, please refer to the Official Rules on the next page. All entries will become the property of Harlequin Enterprises Ltd. and are not returnable.

Please visit www.blazecovermodel.com to download a copy of the Official Entry Form and Publicity Release Form or send a request to one of the addresses below.

Please mail your entry to: **Harlequin Blaze Cover Model Search**

In U.S.A.	In Canada
P.O. Box 9069	P.O. Box 637
Buffalo, NY	Fort Erie, ON
14269-9069	L2A 5X3

No purchase necessary. Contest open to Canadian and U.S. residents who are 18 and over.
Void where prohibited. Contest closes September 30, 2003.

HBCVRMODEL1

HARLEQUIN BLAZE COVER MODEL SEARCH CONTEST 3569 OFFICIAL RULES
NO PURCHASE NECESSARY TO ENTER

1. To enter, submit two (2) 4" x 6" photographs of a boyfriend or spouse (who must be 18 years of age or older) taken no later than three (3) months from the time of entry: a close-up, waist up, shirtless photograph; and a fully clothed, full-length photograph, then, tell us, in 100 words or fewer, why he should be a Harlequin Blaze cover model and how he is romantic. Your complete "entry" must include: (i) your essay, (ii) the Official Entry Form and Publicity Release Form printed below completed and signed by you (as "Entrant"), (iii) the photographs (with your hand-written name, address and phone number, and your model's name, address and phone number on the back of each photograph), and (iv) the Publicity Release Form and Photograph Representation Form printed below completed and signed by your model (as "Model"), and should be sent via first-class mail to either: Harlequin Blaze Cover Model Search Contest 3569, P.O. Box 9069, Buffalo, NY, 14269-9069, or Harlequin Blaze Cover Model Search Contest 3569, P.O. Box 637, Fort Erie, Ontario L2A 5X3. All submissions must be in English and be received no later than September 30, 2003. Limit: one entry per person, household or organization. **Purchase or acceptance of a product offer does not improve your chances of winning.** All entry requirements must be strictly adhered to for eligibility and to ensure fairness among entries.

2. Ten (10) Finalist submissions (photographs and essays) will be selected by a panel of judges consisting of members of the Harlequin editorial, marketing and public relations staff, as well as a representative from Elite Model Management (Toronto) Inc., based on the following criteria:

Aptness/Appropriateness of submitted photographs for a Harlequin Blaze cover—70%
Originality of Essay—20%
Sincerity of Essay—10%

In the event of a tie, duplicate finalists will be selected. The photographs submitted by finalists will be posted on the Harlequin website no later than November 15, 2003 (at www.blazecovermodel.com), and viewers may vote, in rank order, on their favorite(s) to assist in the panel of judges' final determination of the Grand Prize and Runner-up winning entries based on the above judging criteria. All decisions of the judges are final.

3. All entries become the property of Harlequin Enterprises Ltd. and none will be returned. Any entry may be used for future promotional purposes. Elite Model Management (Toronto) Inc. and/or its partners, subsidiaries and affiliates operating as "Elite Model Management" will have access to all entries including all personal information, and may contact any Entrant and/or Model in its sole discretion for their own business purposes. Harlequin and Elite Model Management (Toronto) Inc. are separate entities with no legal association or partnership whatsoever having no power to bind or obligate the other or create any expressed or implied obligation or responsibility on behalf of the other, such that Harlequin shall not be responsible in any way for any acts or omissions of Elite Model Management (Toronto) Inc. or its partners, subsidiaries and affiliates in connection with the Contest or otherwise and Elite Model Management shall not be responsible in any way for any acts or omissions of Harlequin or its partners, subsidiaries and affiliates in connection with the contest or otherwise.

4. All Entrants and Models must be residents of the U.S. or Canada, be 18 years of age or older, and have no prior criminal convictions. The contest is not open to any Model that is a professional model and/or actor in any capacity at the time of the entry. Contest void wherever prohibited by law; all applicable laws and regulations apply. Any litigation within the Province of Quebec regarding the conduct or organization of a publicity contest may be submitted to the Régie des alcools, des courses et des jeux for a ruling, and any litigation regarding the awarding of a prize may be submitted to the Régie only for the purpose of helping the parties reach a settlement. Employees and immediate family members of Harlequin Enterprises Ltd., D.L. Blair, Inc., Elite Model Management (Toronto) Inc. and their parents, affiliates, subsidiaries and all other agencies, entities and persons connected with the use, marketing or conduct of this Contest are not eligible to enter. Acceptance of any prize offered constitutes permission to use Entrants' and Models' names, essay submissions, photographs or other likenesses for the purposes of advertising, trade, publication and promotion on behalf of Harlequin Enterprises Ltd., its parent, affiliates, subsidiaries, assigns and other authorized entities involved in the judging and promotion of the contest without further compensation to any Entrant or Model, unless prohibited by law.

5. Finalists will be determined no later than October 30, 2003. Prize Winners will be determined no later than January 31, 2004. Grand Prize Winners (consisting of winning Entrant and Model) will be required to sign and return Affidavit of Eligibility/Release of Liability and Model Release forms within thirty (30) days of notification. Non-compliance with this requirement and within the specified time period will result in disqualification and an alternate will be selected. Any prize notification returned as undeliverable will result in the awarding of the prize to an alternate set of winners. All travelers (or parent/legal guardian of a minor) must execute the Affidavit of Eligibility/Release of Liability prior to ticketing and must possess required travel documents (e.g. valid photo ID) where applicable. Travel dates specified by Sponsor but no later than May 30, 2004.

6. Prizes: One (1) Grand Prize—the opportunity for the Model to appear on the cover of a paperback book from the Harlequin Blaze series, and a 3 day/2 night trip for two (Entrant and Model) to New York, NY for the photo shoot of Model which includes round-trip coach air transportation from the commercial airport nearest the winning Entrant's home to New York, NY (or, in lieu of air transportation, $100 cash payable to Entrant and Model, if the winning Entrant's home is within 250 miles of New York, NY), hotel accommodations (double occupancy) at the Plaza Hotel and $500 cash spending money payable to Entrant and Model, (approximate prize value: $8,000), and one (1) Runner-up Prize of $200 cash payable to Entrant and Model for a romantic dinner for two (approximate prize value: $200). Prizes are valued in U.S. currency. Prizes consist of only those items listed as part of the prize. No substitution of prize(s) permitted by winners. All prizes are awarded jointly to the Entrant and Model of the winning entries, and are not severable - prizes and obligations may not be assigned or transferred. Any change to the Entrant and/or Model of the winning entries will result in disqualification and an alternate will be selected. Taxes on prize are the sole responsibility of winners. Any and all expenses and/or items not specifically described as part of the prize are the sole responsibility of winners. Harlequin Enterprises Ltd. and D.L. Blair, Inc., their parents, affiliates, subsidiaries are not responsible for errors in printing of Contest entries and/or game pieces. No responsibility is assumed for lost, stolen, late, illegible, incomplete, inaccurate, non-delivered, postage due or misdirected mail or entries. In the event of printing or other errors which may result in unintended prize values or duplication of prizes, all affected game pieces or entries shall be null and void.

7. Winners will be notified by mail. For winners' list (available after March 31, 2004), send a self-addressed, stamped envelope to: Harlequin Blaze Cover Model Search Contest 3569 Winners, P.O. Box 4200, Blair, NE 68009-4200, or refer to the Harlequin website (at www.blazecovermodel.com).

Contest sponsored by Harlequin Enterprises Ltd., P.O. Box 9042, Buffalo, NY 14269-9042.

HBCVRMODEL2

HARLEQUIN®
INTRIGUE®

When a wealthy family is torn apart by greed
and murder, two couples must protect the
inheritance—and the lives—of two orphans.

Only their love can save…

THE COLLINGWOOD HEIRS

a new series by

JOYCE SULLIVAN

THE BUTLER'S DAUGHTER
August 2003

Reclusive millionaire Hunter Sinclair would do anything
to protect his godson from a killer—even marry
a woman he'd never met.

OPERATION BASSINET
September 2003

Detective Mitch Halloran discovered the baby switch.
But how could he tell the little girl's innocent mother…?

Available at your favorite retail outlet.

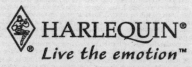

HARLEQUIN®
Live the emotion™

Visit us at www.eHarlequin.com

HICHAST